Believe!

The Mysterious Christmas Farm

An Inexplicable Tale of Wonder

Cynthia J Dueringer

Ridiculous Life Publishing
Lenexa, Kansas
2022

Dedication

To my three children, Monica, Adrienne, and Terrence,
who know how much I love them.
My three kids have given me a thousand reasons to
Believe!

About the Author

I am delighted to hear from my readers. You can contact me at my website. You will also find information about me, some writing samples, essays, and silly poems that you can read for FREE. You can also buy my books 📚…not free. I will also have book-author gift kits you can purchase while they last. Check it out. I feel encouraged when I get web traffic. My website:

cynthiajdueringer-author.com

Or you can shoot me an email: ✉

cynthiajdueringer@gmail.com

I try to reply to emails as quickly as I can.

Table of Contents

Chapter 1 - Hitching a Ride 1

Chapter 2 - Lovely Rita? 4

Chapter 3 – Safe! At Home 8

Chapter 4 - The Collection 10

Chapter 5 – Mother Rules 13

Chapter 6 – Those Ding-Dong Church Bells 15

Chapter 7 – Reasons for Razzies........................ 20

Chapter 8 – Clinical Trials 23

Chapter 9 – A Cuppa Tea.................................. 26

Chapter 10 – Sloppy Joe's 33

Chapter 11 – Pastor-ized 40

Chapter 12 – Hanging with Joe.......................... 45

Chapter 13 – Walking and Wishing 48

Chapter 14 – Farm House Secrets 52

Chapter 15 – Invitation 55

Chapter 16 – Telling Tales 58

Chapter 17 – Pick Up Lines 65

Chapter 18 – Bumpy Roads 68

Chapter 19 – Lost in Snow Where........................ 73

Chapter 20 – Light in the Darkness..................... 78

Chapter 21 - The Farmer and his Wife.................. 82

Chapter 22 – No Room in the Inn 85

Chapter 23 – Accommodating Accommodations..... 90

Chapter 24 – Count Your Blessings 94

Chapter 25 – What Child is This? 96

Chapter 26 – Meanwhile, Back at the House 99

Chapter 27 – Incoming! 102

Chapter 28 – Bearing Gifts..............................107

Chapter 29 – Santa Clauses Coming to Town 110

Chapter 30 – Cradle of Civilization 114

Chapter 31 – Grandma Pokes Around.................118

Chapter 32 – Grandma Off her Rocker.................121

Chapter 33 – Gabe's Reassuring Words 124

Chapter 34 – Sweet Dreams 129

Chapter 35 – Meanwhile, Back at the House Pt2 ..131

Chapter 36 – The Grand Christmas Feast............135

Chapter 37 – Mysterious Gabe 140

Chapter 38 – Saying Goodbye is Hard 145

Chapter 39 – The Road Back to Reality................150

Chapter 40 – Behind the Double-Doors 155

Chapter 41 - Ashes to Ashes, Dust to Dust 159

Chapter 42 – Gabe 167

Epilog 174

Chapter 1

Hitching a Ride

Running from your Problems?

MaryAnn stood in the swirling snow, hopelessly pulling at the edges of her coat, trying to cover herself from the cold. The coat belonged to Aunt Rachel, a slim older lady, making the coat too small for MaryAnn's much larger girth. But on this blustery frozen night, it was better than nothing. She hoped her Aunt would not be angry that she took the coat without asking, but tonight was an emergency. There was no time to get permission about coats.

"Where are you?" MaryAnn chattered quietly to herself as she strained to look down the road and saw nothing but snowy darkness. "You're late!" she griped as she tucked her chin down into her sweatshirt to try to stop the swirling snow from going down her neck. Glancing back to Aunt Rachel's farmhouse, no lights were on so far. "Hurry up, Joe. You gotta get me outta here before Aunt Rachel wakes up."

Although it might seem rather normal for a young girl to want to run off with a guy, MaryAnn is not so normal, and this is not a normal story. It is not what you think at all.

You must first know the whole mystifying tale. Whether you want to believe it or not is up to you.

Let's see, where to begin? Well, let's start in the middle.

It was just a couple of months ago, in the pre-dawn hours that Aunt Rachel unexpectedly found young MaryAnn stumbling up her gravel road. Aunt Rachel knew her farm was almost fifteen miles from town and realized that MaryAnn, nearly eighteen now, was in some serious trouble to have walked that distance on gravel and dirt roads in the dark. Sensing MaryAnn was harboring something deep, Aunt Rachel took the girl in. Then not wanting to overwhelm MaryAnn with an immediate interrogation, Aunt Rachel didn't ask any questions right away knowing she would be asking plenty of questions, but later after MaryAnn had some time to collect herself. Aunt Rachel knew eventually the girl would be willing to talk.

And so it happened a few days later on a dreary late afternoon over coffee and cookies that Aunt Rachel casually asked MaryAnn what happened that she decided to walk all the way to her farm at night instead of simply calling for her to pick her up. It took a little coaxing, but after some cautious nudging, MaryAnn finally opened up, but just a little.

With a lot of hesitation in her story that Aunt Rachel thought was a bit suspicious, MaryAnn said she left home because of her terrible habit of stopping at the corner market and loading up with chips, snack cakes, and a few candy bars to binge on while watching old TV shows when her mother went out. And her mother went out a lot. MaryAnn explained that the bounty from the market and the mind-numbing TV programs helped her deal with her fears and anxieties of what lies ahead. She admitted that the peace was brief, only lasting until there was nothing left but empty wrappers, crumbs, and the final credits. Then the worries came rushing back, including extra poundage, which made her mother rant at her more than ever about her weight.

Aunt Rachel knew about MaryAnn's life-long chronic eating issues and was wise enough to know that her snacking was not a new problem. MaryAnn's real problem, from MaryAnn's accidental mention of anxieties and worries in their conversation, was something else. Aunt Rachel knew the problem was deeper and bigger, much bigger. Something else was bothering MaryAnn much more than mere snacking and her mother's nagging.

Now MaryAnn knew she could always talk to Aunt Rachel about anything. She was the only person MaryAnn knew that could possibly understand her unraveling. When things got bad at home, MaryAnn would call Aunt Rachel and she would drop everything to pick up MaryAnn. The two would talk away the afternoon. MaryAnn always felt better after a long conversation as Aunt Rachel could get to the heart of the matter, sorting everything out, and making even the worst problems seem manageable.

So Aunt Rachel was very wise and MaryAnn knew it, suspecting that Aunt Rachel wasn't buying her song and dance of snacking too much and arguing with her mother. MaryAnn wondered if she could ever tell Aunt Rachel the real truth. Would Aunt Rachel understand the formidable situation MaryAnn was facing now? MaryAnn wasn't sure that this time Aunt Rachel would grasp the seriousness of her current situation because, until this latest over-whelming dilemma, most of MaryAnn's problems were always with her mother.

*   *   *

Chapter 2

Lovely Rita?
Meet her Maid

*E*verything started years ago with Rita, MaryAnn's mother. Rita was Aunt Rachel's younger sister by nearly nine years, and Aunt Rachel saw trouble brewing shortly after Rita married very young and got pregnant right away. Rita, always overly concerned about her looks, didn't want anyone to see her with her belly bloated out with the baby, so she left her husband during the last two months of the pregnancy to live with her mother on the other side of the county line until the baby was born. And it was a good thing because Rita wasn't all that interested in being a mother after the baby came. But Grandma Ruth, Rita and Rachel's mother, was immediately smitten with the little one and doted on little baby MaryAnn while Rita returned to town to try to put her marriage back together. And to keep her appointments with the hairdresser, nail salon, local spa, and the town cocktail lounges.

Grandma Ruth loved having baby MaryAnn around, and Rita loved not having her lifestyle cramped with baby care and maintenance. She had no tolerance for splattered strained peas, baby barf, or the smell of diaper contents. Rita had zero patience to sit and hold a bottle unless it was gin, so Rita made chronic excuses to get back to town. Grandma Ruth didn't mind Rita's running around as she was happy caring for MaryAnn. Grandma Ruth was so delighted with the baby's sunshine-happy personality that she started calling her Merry-MaryAnn. It was all weird and awkward, to say the least, but in spite of the lopsidedness in the family, things were going pretty well for Merry MaryAnn.

But not for long.

After MaryAnn's fourth birthday, that's when things started to go haywire. It began when MaryAnn's father tired of Rita's drinking and spending hours at the Brown Lobster Lounge or Jerry's Gin Joint. Eventually, after many intense arguments about Rita's lifestyle, MaryAnn's father moved out. That suited Rita just fine. With her child at her mother's and her husband gone, Rita had no responsibilities to anyone. She could socialize and drink as she pleased. No one was sure what Rita did more of, socializing or drinking. The talk around town was that it was a tie.

It wasn't long before her divorce was final and Rita was thrilled. Rita drank and partied her carefree days and evenings away. Then, after a very few months of her devil-may-care play time, Rita's freedom came to a screeching halt because Grandma Ruth suddenly became very ill and died quickly after. Rita had no choice after that. She was forced to take her daughter back to town with her and make a place in her freestyle life for a four-year-old. The sting of it caused Rita deep resentment toward a little girl in pigtails. Rita was not aware that eventually, she would be paying a penalty for her loose lifestyle and the disregard of little Merry-MaryAnn.

Little Merry MaryAnn never really got over the sudden departure of her Grandma Ruth, and going to live with her mother was a rude shock. As a divorcee, Rita wanted to be out socializing, and a four-year-old disrupted those plans. Rita hired sitters or waited for MaryAnn to fall asleep before leaving the house and going out to party. A once happy-go-lucky little girl became withdrawn and miserable. She was no longer "merry". Many times MaryAnn would wake at night and find herself alone in the house. She was afraid in the dark by herself and would cry for her grandmother.

So now you know that Rita was the opposite of her loving mother Ruth and compassionate sister Rachel. Rita was obnoxious, arrogant, domineering, and vain....crazy vain. She was always getting her hair done, nails done, facials done, and plenty of spa treatments done. Anything she could have done, was done. She ordered lots of lacy things to push stuff up or smash it down as needed. Dresses were shortened and cleavage was accented. She spent more money on her own personal upkeep than she spent on utilities justifying the expense to herself that if she looked more glamorous, she would be respected by the people in the town. She wanted that respect because she could feel the burn of the town's people that snubbed her. It was not only Rita's vanity that got her the cold shoulder, it was also her crass personality and boozy lifestyle. It all came down to Rita being disliked by most of the town except for Sally, the owner of the Hair Pin Curves salon, Michele, the owner of the Omm Depot Day Spa, and the bartenders at The Brown Lobster Lounge and Jerry's Gin Joint.

Needless to say, but we will say it anyway, Rita was not family oriented. So as MaryAnn grew, Rita considered her little daughter chubby, homely, and useless baggage that took up too much of her time when Rita had so many "self-care" appointments and social engagements to keep.

As months and years passed, Rita tried to hide her embarrassment at what she considered her daughter's homely looks. For the first days of elementary school, she over-dressed her daughter. She assumed pretty dresses and frilly ribbons in her hair would make her popular. But kids are kids. The rest of the kids showed up to school in jeans and t-shirts.

By junior high, MaryAnn was embarrassed by the way

her mother made her dress, so she kept a gray hoodie in her locker that she picked out of the lost-and-found. She would wear it over her clothes and use the hood to cover her out-of-whack hair. MaryAnn thought she was hiding her clothes and hair, but the kids just thought she was strange.

Through her school years, she became withdrawn and painfully shy. Her mother's chronic criticism eroded her teen years, and the constant belittling for being slightly overweight wore MaryAnn down. The trifecta of a teenager's grief is being plain, chunky, and shy and MaryAnn was a composite of all three. The other kids weren't taunting her or physically abusive, but they made it clear they didn't want her company. She was an oddity to them. She was an outcast.

With no friends of her own and her ridiculous mother that had begun to treat her as a Cinderella-maid to do many of the household chores, her life was lonely and difficult. Snacking was her only relief, and as you already know, it was causing more weight gain which wasn't helping her relationship with her mother.

Suppertime for MaryAnn became the most unpleasant time of day. One of her daily chores was to start supper after school so it would be almost ready when Rita decided to come home. As soon as her mother came swishing in the door, she would start griping at MaryAnn about losing weight if she ever wanted friends. The drumming of that at every dinner meal was making MaryAnn hate dinner. She would eat less at the table to shut her mother up, and then later, fill up on junk food that she rat-holed in her "safe room".

*   *   *

Chapter 3

Safe! At Home

A safe room? MaryAnn had a safe room, you ask?

Yes, she did. THE Safe Room.

Well, actually, it was an attic space, but for MaryAnn it was a place to feel safe and reasonably relaxed. So she called it her safe room. It is unfortunate that MaryAnn felt a need to have a safe room. That is another story you need to know.

The attic space was accessed by a small door at the back of MaryAnn's closet that led to the stuffy third-floor attic in their century-old home, and MaryAnn had worn a path to it.

The attic was a place to be well out of her mother's way as it was best to make herself scarce to escape her mother's chronic criticism and excessive drinking. The attic was perfect to be alone and hassle-free. Above all, the attic was a handy place to conceal the accumulation of emergency snacks and to hide things she knew her mother would not approve of.

MaryAnn found welcome relief in the quiet of the attic. She had tricked it out with a few comforting odds and ends like an old rug, a big beanbag chair, and her grandmother's boudoir lamp. On a small vintage dresser lived a few favorite photos of her father, Grandma Ruth, and Aunt Rachel....but none of her mother. The dresser had three little drawers, handy for hiding snacks and keeping a few other personal secrets.

It was reasonably clean, plenty dry, and not too stuffy.

But there, in the middle of the attic floor was...space. Space enough for The Collection.

*   *   *

Chapter 4

The Collection

The Profits of Prophets

There was never a particular starting point of MaryAnn's collection that anyone could recall, but because MaryAnn always felt so depressed and alone she would pray from time to time when she was in her attic space. As time went on, her praying time increased as did her prayers. Eventually, she began to feel as though her prayers were not being answered and praying was hopeless.

MaryAnn understood that the prayers her Grandmother taught her were just to go to sleep peacefully and did not cover her requests for having a friend, losing some weight, and hoping her mother would stop drinking.

Then it happened. It began slowly. MaryAnn started to bring home religious trinkets thinking it would surely increase the power of her prayers. If there was more strength to her prayers using the figurines and charms maybe she'd finally get some results.

At first, the collection consisted of the familiar figures she got at garage sales and thrift shops around town, starting with a partial nativity set. Soon she had collected crosses, Jesus figures, and a few Mother Mary trinkets. Then she learned about other faiths and what they prayed to through television, movies, and books. Since her mother never bothered to go to church, MaryAnn didn't know which faith was most powerful. So eventually, the religion did not matter. She collected figures from as many faiths as she could, trying to cover all the bases, hoping they would increase the chances of her prayers being answered.

On a wooden wire spool set up to use as a table, her little menagerie grew. The small religious figures and trinkets included a small happy Buddha, a figure of Saint Francis holding a little lamb, a blue ceramic Krishna, a plastic toy Torah, an eagle feather, a crucifix of Jesus, a little Menorah, a Ganesh souvenir, a New York Subway token, a couple of ceramic cherubs, a rosary with a few beads missing, and a couple of angels. A few things she wasn't sure were religious, but she collected them just in case. Anything with angel wings was included, and for good luck, she picked up a rabbit's foot keychain and a penny she found in the street. She had a four-leaf clover once, but it dried up and blew off the table someplace when she opened the attic door too quickly.

Of all the trinkets, her most cherished item was a small cheap plastic glow-in-the-dark cross her grandmother gave her when she was very small. Her grandmother made a nighttime ritual of putting the cross under a lamp light while getting MaryAnn ready for bed. When MaryAnn was settled in bed, her grandmother would turn out the lights, and by the glow of the cross, Grandma Ruth would say nighttime prayers with MaryAnn.

And now, so many years later, MaryAnn would leave the cross in the attic window all day then in the quiet of the evening she would place it in the middle of her collection and pray in front of it all, asking for forgiveness for eating, forgiveness for hating her mother, and endlessly asking for the miracle of a good friendship or true love. But so far, her prayers had been ignored by the redeemers of prayer requests and seemingly unheard by the conglomeration of plastic and ceramic prophets, gods, and saints on the spool table.

Considering her array of religious knick-knacks, she became discouraged that her prayers were still not being answered. She assumed it was because she simply didn't deserve it. She could not see where she did anything worthy of receiving prayer gifts. She also wondered if the faiths were punishing her for not being a church member anywhere. Maybe that mattered. She also considered maybe the different representations of religions cancelled each other out. Or maybe true faith eluded her because there were proper rituals assigned to the various figurines and statues that she didn't know.

The one thing MaryAnn did know was that her life was increasingly miserable, so she kept praying. If nothing else, she prayed for a good friend. She didn't think it was too much to ask.

*   *   *

Chapter 5

Mother Rules

*M*aryAnn's mother had some concerns about MaryAnn not having any friends. She would nag MaryAnn to go for walks and to take exercise seriously to lose some weight, then maybe she'd find some friends. On warm summer days, if her mother had a few drinks in her, she'd swat MaryAnn's bare legs with a flyswatter to get her moving faster. MaryAnn resented her mother more each day.

Of course, MaryAnn tried to develop a friend or two and at least attempted to blend in with the other kids. She'd been saving up some of her babysitting money to buy a decent pair of jeans to wear instead of the ridiculous skirts and dresses. Still, all of her mother's fat-nagging upset MaryAnn more and more, causing her to funnel her meager savings into more snacks to sneak up to the attic, where she could eat in secret. She realized that snacking only momentarily soothed her anger and eventually added to her weight, but she couldn't deal with the feeling of rejection from every direction in any other way. MaryAnn spent hours up in the quiet attic space of the old house, and her mother was fine with that. The less Rita saw MaryAnn, the better she liked it.

At almost eighteen now, MaryAnn knew in another half year, she'd be able to be independent of her mother and knew that as soon as she was out of school, she'd leave her mother and the gossipy town just as fast as her father did. Let the town talk. Knowing her mother was the town's most gossiped-about resident, she knew leaving would create more gossip about her mother. MaryAnn enjoyed thinking about the sweet revenge and yet secretly hated that she felt that way. There was no question that the town's folk would descend on a juicy tidbit about Rita, especially if MaryAnn had a huge secret and the secret got out.

And as you well know, secrets always have a way of getting out.

So now you know why Aunt Rachel's farm was a warm and welcoming place for MaryAnn to escape to because Aunt Rachel was the sole person on the planet that could be trusted to keep the secrets.

*   *   *

Chapter 6

Those Ding-Dong Church Bells

The Call Came

$\mathcal{S}$o now that you know MaryAnn's situation, you may be wondering what led up to MaryAnn standing in the snow in front of Aunt Rachel's farm, waiting for a ride to get away from what seemed to be a safe haven.

It was the church bells. This may seem ridiculous but read on.

For many years in the quiet of the attic, MaryAnn could always hear church bells on Sunday morning coming from the center of town. When her mother slept in, MaryAnn would go for a morning walk heading toward the peal of the bells. As she neared the little white clapboard chapel, she could hear the rich sound of the organ playing church music inside and watched people and their families gathering to go in. A bit later, they filed out, all smiling; the families together, shaking hands with the minister while the bells happily rang. She ached to have a family like that and to attend the church. Instead, she'd go back to the house and cringe when her mother yelled at her about a variety of things until she could sneak back up to the quiet of the attic, then pray to the conglomeration of icons in a desperate attempt to end the loneliness she felt.

Then one day, something strange about that chapel

happened. While she was leaving school, she felt the other kids went out of their way to block her exit. Although no one bumped her or nudged her, their conduct just seemed more antagonistic than the usual exit treatment. It so troubled her that she felt the stinging harbinger of tears as she left the building and increased her pace to get away from everyone. Frustrated with the town and feeling bummed about life, MaryAnn hurried toward home. Why me, she wondered. I've never harmed anyone! I've never even cussed at anyone...well, out loud anyway. She always remembered what her grandmother told her, to be friendly and do unto others. And she dutifully tried.

As she got farther from school, she slowed her pace and began to consider the option of running away. She discussed with herself where she could possibly go at her age without having any money. It was at that very moment that MaryAnn felt an overwhelming compulsion to turn and walk to the church. She argued with her compulsion because she knew she had no business at the church but found herself on the sidewalk in front of it. MaryAnn was aware that she was now closer to the church than she'd ever been before, just a few feet from the big wooden double doors. Her sense of urgency to enter the church battled with her fears of intruding on what goes on inside. She dared to walk up to the big doors taking a few moments to gather the courage to test the door handles. Surely they would be locked. With just a light tug on one of the brass handles, she surprisingly found it unlocked. Then with a timid cautious pull on one of the doors, it opened a bit to reveal just a peek of the inside. When she didn't see or hear anyone, she quietly slipped in, trying to make herself as small and as insignificant as possible.

She quickly glanced around to see if she interrupted anything or anyone, her wide eyes shifting from side to side like a vintage kitty-cat wall clock to take it all in. She was immediately overcome by the rich woodwork, the rows of benches, and the simple altar with the obligatory cross of Jesus that was nearly identical to one in her menagerie. Small stained glass windows lined the sides of the church, letting in the afternoon light in shafts of blue, green, gold, and red streaking and splashing around the sanctuary. It felt spiritual just standing there and looking. She stepped into the nearest pew, sat, and bowed her head, here, where she felt a moving sense of reverence in the church's atmosphere, hoping that just maybe her prayers will be heard from this sacred place.

"Please, God," she whispered so quietly, "please help me find someone that will love me and someone I can love with all my heart. Amen."

She sat there in reflective peace for some time, hoping for a miracle. After a few minutes, she didn't feel any different or that anything was happening, so she decided to get home. As she stood to leave, she abruptly tripped on the aisle runner. Grabbing at the edge of the pew to avoid falling, she knocked a stack of hymnals off the seat, making a racket that echoed all over the little peaceful sanctuary. Embarrassed and upset at her clumsiness, she stooped to re-stack the books when an extra hand showed up to help.

"Are you okay?" a young man asked her.

MaryAnn looked up and felt the sting of being so gawky, screwing up, and worse, being found out that she sneaked into the church, and by a nice young man, no less. She didn't respond to his question. She just returned to re-stacking the hymnals.

The young man didn't push for details. He simply began to help her return the books to the seat of the pew. When it was all stacked up nicely, he said in a light-hearted manner, "There we are, our Steeple of Song," and he extended his hand to help her up.

MaryAnn looked at his hand, and thoughts blew through her head about accepting it or not. First, she considered it was a nice gesture to help her get up like a lady, then she considered declining his help and possibly stumbling and landing on her face. She chose to accept the gesture while apologizing. "I'm sorry to have disturbed you." She looked around and didn't see anyone else to apologize to.

"It is okay," he said. I'm glad you felt you could come here when you needed some time to pray, reflect, or look for answers." He was trying to coax her to talk, maybe share her troubles. "Are you from around here?"

She didn't answer right away. She couldn't because all she could think of was how sweaty her hand was and how it felt when his hand touched hers. She felt embarrassingly uncomfortable, yet in a small way, it made her feel momentarily accepted as normal. She was shocked he didn't withdraw even though he could see how homely and chubby she was. His hand felt warm and strong, especially when she considered how mushy her hands undoubtedly felt. When she was righted, she swept imaginary dust off her thighs with her hands and looked around the chapel as though the answer to his question would be written on the wall somewhere. It took a few seconds, but she finally formulated a response.

"Yes. I've lived here since I was four or five." She kept nervously sweeping the imaginary dust from her backside.

He could see she was shy or troubled or both. Either way, he felt a need to help ease her discomfort.

"Oh. So you live nearby? Well, that's good. You must be a neighbor then. We must have been missing each other. I've been here since I was in elementary school, so a dozen or so years now, but I don't recall seeing you in school."

MaryAnn really didn't want to have this conversation. But she needed to be polite. "I'm still in school," she said in a disappointed whisper.

He was surprised. She looked older and like the weight of the world was resting on her shoulders. "Oh, I'm sorry.

I didn't mean to invade on your personal privacy," he said, nearly kicking himself for over-stepping this young lady's boundaries.

"It's okay," she said, wanting to alleviate his concerns but also wanting to alleviate herself from the chapel right now, or sooner. "I have to go. I can't be late." She made up the excuse so she wouldn't have to continue the prodding conversation, then stepped around him, heading to the chapel doors.

"My name is Joe," he spoke in her direction, hoping it would elicit her name. When it looked like she wasn't going to reply, he added, "You are welcome to come in anytime. We'll leave you to your peace if you want or lead you in prayer. There are no rules to sit in the chapel."

MaryAnn kept walking but did say thank you and left. Joe watched her until the door closer silently pulled the door shut.

Walking home, MaryAnn felt both ridiculous for sneaking into the church and worse about knocking over the stack of books. She was curious about the young man though, as he was wearing a sweatshirt and loose jeans. She had never seen him around the church on the mornings she went to hear the church bells. Was he a maintenance guy? The choir director? A floor polisher? A hearse driver? Not actually remembering what he looked like, she was aware that he had a peaceful nature about him with a sincere caring voice.

*   *   *

Chapter 7

Reasons for Razzies

What is a Razzie Anyway?

*A*ll MaryAnn's thoughts about the chapel and the young man vaporized when she got home and walked into the house. It reeked of hair spray, nail polishes, and salon chemicals. As MaryAnn entered the living room, her mother was sitting in her comfy chair, her feet on the footstool with cotton threaded between her toes like fuzzy snakes, an eye mask on her face that blotted out her vision while holding a cocktail in her hand. A gaudy charm bracelet jingled with every sip of her drink.

Holy cow, MaryAnn thought, mother had her weekly overhaul at maintaining her youth. MaryAnn knew that depending on the results would depend on her mother's mood, and today seemed, thankfully, middle of the road, or maybe she'd already moved to her second hi-ball.

"Where have you been, you pathetic excuse for a daughter?" Rita shouted into the air. "You were supposed to start dinner before I got home. I can't be sticking my hands in ground beef with my fresh nail polish, and I can't have the stench of onions sticking to my hair. I need my dinner early because I have to go out later."

MaryAnn trudged back to the kitchen to start some dinner. Her mother required meatloaf once a week, and it was MaryAnn's job to make it from scratch.

"I asked you, where have you been?" her mother shouted from the living room, becoming more agitated.

"I went for a walk. You've been griping about me getting exercise, so I went for a walk around town."

"I wish you wouldn't be walking in town. Can't you walk on the outer roads so nobody can see you?" Rita took a good gulp of her hi-ball while MaryAnn gritted her teeth in frustration at her mother's toxic comment.

MaryAnn slapped dinner together, adding more salt to the meatloaf than necessary, hoping it might add to her mother's water weight which would drive her crazy when she stepped on the scale. Her mother checked her weight at least three or four times a day, consumed with her own vanity. All the time and money her mother spent on the upkeep, MaryAnn thought she should spend some of it on a shrink's couch.

After finishing cleaning up dinner, she was relieved to head up to her room and into the attic so she could relax. Her mother would never venture into the attic. She was afraid of bats and bugs, but so far, MaryAnn had never seen any. But just in case, to keep her space private, she'd use an old piece of a two-by-four to bang on the wall studs and floors, then yell down to her mother that she got rid of another bat. Problem solved.

This evening was chilly, so MaryAnn grabbed a quilt before snuggling up to read for a while. She loved reading romance novels and of the handsome men that eventually fell in love with the heroine. She wished she could be the heroine of her own romance just once. And who doesn't? She'd been buying the romance paperbacks at the thrift store, hiding them in the dresser drawer, then donating them back so her mother wouldn't see what she was reading instead of doing homework. She had a few Razzies snack cakes hidden in another drawer for an emergency, and after the church fiasco earlier in the day, she dug one out of its hiding place. After carefully unwrapping it, she smelled it from end to end like a fine Cuban cigar. "Mmmm, sooo good," she said to the cake, loving the sweet raspberry and coconut coating and the vanilla cake inside. It helped neutralize the acid tongue of her mother.

While picking off pieces of Razzie and reading her romance, her mind trailed off to the guy at the chapel. He actually talked to her instead of at her. Who was he? Was he handsome? Did he have hair? He said his name was Joe, and he'd been in town for years, but she had never heard of him. He wasn't the pastor either. She'd seen the much older, gray-haired pastor Sundays after church standing by the doorway, shaking hands with the patrons. So who was this Joe guy? She lost her place in the book while the curiosity of the young man kept penetrating her thoughts when she suddenly felt that the items on the spool table seemed to be talking to her, urging her to go back to the chapel. She didn't want to because she felt so stupid, but she also felt like something else was in the air. It was like a nudge, a pull, or maybe a yank, but something on that spool was urging her to return to the church.

*   *   *

Chapter 8

Clinical Trials

That Nagging Nausea

*M*aryAnn didn't go to school the following day. She wasn't feeling well again. "I shouldn't have eaten two packages of Razzies last night." She criticized herself, knowing she'd felt lousy the past few weeks after eating so much junk. She knew her anger with her mother and stress about the kids at school were gnawing at her gut. Her grandmother died quite suddenly from a problem in her stomach, so MaryAnn grew concerned enough about her stomach trouble to head to the town free clinic shortly after her mother left for the day.

An older gray-haired woman in maroon scrubs with a piece of masking tape across her chest with Florence written on it in magic marker welcomed MaryAnn as she came in. Only one other person sat in the waiting area, an elderly man that was hopelessly trying to stifle a cough. Florence finally called his name, "Elmer, the PA will see you now," then escorted the old man to a room in the back. MaryAnn heard the exam room door close and some muffled talking. Florence returned and handed MaryAnn some papers to fill out with the usual information and a description of the problem. She filled them out and handed them back to Florence. As Florence checked the papers, MaryAnn asked her, "What is a PA?" Florence explained it was a physician's assistant. The clinic only had an MD oversight in severe cases. Anything else the PA could manage. MaryAnn sat back down and contemplated leaving as her stomach seemed to be feeling better, but Florence called her name and escorted her to another room in the back. Florence took her vitals, wrote down the scores, and asked her what the problem was. MaryAnn explained the nausea and about her grandmother dying quickly from similar symptoms. Florence noted it all and told her the PA would be with her shortly, leaving MaryAnn alone in the little room. MaryAnn was looking around at the various posters and equipment when the PA knocked on the door making MaryAnn jump.

Once again, MaryAnn explained the symptoms to the PA. She listened nicely and asked a few more questions while doing a cursory physical exam. The PA took a few blood samples and had her pee in a cup, then said she'd be back in a few minutes, she was going to run tests. MaryAnn's heart racing as she worried about what the result would be. Was her health in danger? Was her stomach going to explode soon? Was she going to die like her grandmother? After what seemed like forever, the PA returned with Florence, ramping up MaryAnn's fears. Were they going to tag-team her to tell her she was going to die?

"MaryAnn," the PA began, "it isn't quite clear, but it appears you might be pregnant." MaryAnn's head began to spin. She suddenly felt weak and about to pass out. Florence noticed and helped MaryAnn off the exam table and into a chair while the PA mentioned to MaryAnn that since she was not eighteen that her parents would be consulted. Florence handed MaryAnn another clipboard with more paperwork, but MaryAnn wasn't interested in filling out anything else. She felt that this was baloney. There wasn't a guy in the entire county that would have wanted to sleep with her or even a guy *out* of the county. She'd never had relations with anyone. She never had a date or even spent time with a guy. This had to be some crazy mistake. She tried to explain to Florence and the PA that this was impossible.

"Oh, many young girls your age say the same thing," Florence said, but not in a condescending way. She said it like her grandmother would have, concerned and caring. MaryAnn begged them not to tell her mother, as things were not good in the home department. She explained how her mother dumped her at her grandmother's until her grandmother died. She mentioned her mother spent a lot of time at local cocktail lounges, and news like this, true or not, would get MaryAnn kicked out of the house or drive her mother to drink more - or both.

Florence looked again at the paperwork and asked MaryAnn who her mother was, as her name didn't sound familiar for such a small town. MaryAnn explained that her father left, and when the divorce was done, her mother reverted back to her maiden name, but she kept her father's name. When MaryAnn mentioned her mother was Rita Blackmost, Florence scowled. "Oh, yes, I know who that is. She was brought to the clinic a few times after passing out at the Brown Lobster or Jerry's Gin Joint. Oh my dear, yes, you do have a difficult mother," Florence confessed. Florence and the PA stepped out into the hall and MaryAnn could hear their hushed voices discussing something.

When they came back, Florence calmed everyone, saying they'd worry about it later in case the test was a mistake. Florence did the math and calculated that MaryAnn would probably be 18 before the baby was born *if* it was a pregnancy and not some crazy mix-up. They'd just wait it out until MaryAnn's birthday.

*　　*　　*

Chapter 9

A Cuppa Tea

And a Regular Joe

MaryAnn left the clinic to head home with a sickening blizzard of stuff going on in her head and another blizzard going on in her stomach. She'd never be able to explain this to her mother if it was true. How could it be true? She couldn't even explain it to herself. She knew there'd never been a guy. Did someone drug her? When? She was always at home or at school. Surely she would have known or remembered something about it. She knew she never did anything like that, so it had to be a tumor....or cancer!! She stopped near a tree and threw up, then started to cry. She felt so alone, lost, and scared.

Tears continued to fall, and her nose ran, and after a few dry heaves, a hand came before her with a couple of tissues in it. She thanked the person, then wiped her mouth and blew her nose to clean up a bit. When she looked up, it was Joe from the church. His hand rescued her again. He asked her if she was okay.

"I don't know," she said. "I just don't know."

Joe saw the tears of fear in her eyes. "Come with me," he told her and extended his hand. She wouldn't take his hand but nodded okay. He walked slowly to allow her a comfortable pace assuming she had the flu or something.

He led her a block over to the chapel, and when MaryAnn saw the little church, she was conflicted about it now. If what the people at the clinic told her was true, had she broken some commandment? Did she somehow do something and have no memory of it at all? Was it possible? She had no one to confide in, and in a small town, you simply don't talk about your troubles unless you want it to be broadcast all over town.

Joe opened the chapel doors and led MaryAnn in. The doors closed silently, but their footsteps echoed in the chapel as he led her up the aisle and around the side of the altar into a small hallway, down a short flight of steps, then into a very small cozy, lamp-lit office. "Have a seat," he told her and pointed to the lone chair. It was upholstered and it rocked to boot. MaryAnn loved rocking chairs, so she sat and rocked until her upset stomach convinced her to stop. Joe asked her if she'd like some hot chamomile tea. She looked at him blankly. He said it would calm her. She nodded. She'd never had the tea before, but something hot right now would feel good on her raw throat from the acid barf, and maybe it would calm her stomach.

Joe left the office to get the tea leaving MaryAnn to look around. He had a number of books on a small shelf, most were about helping people, but others were psychology books, books on faith, two paperback books on writing jokes, and an old copy of a town phone book. There was a cross on the wall behind his desk and stacks of papers on the desk in a big confused mess. Joe came back with a little tray that had two mugs and a teapot wearing a silly tea cozy that was in the shape of a chicken wearing a purple vest with pink hearts. He poured two mugs and handed one to MaryAnn. "It's hot, be careful," he warned her.

She sipped a bit, swallowed, and finally spoke a full sentence. "This feels good."

"I know," he said. "That's why I drink it often, and it'll

take the edge off the nerves. Hope it works for you."

MaryAnn nodded, adding, "I hope it works too. It doesn't taste very good. It tastes kind of like throwing grass clippings in hot water."

Joe smiled widely at her joke and chuckled a bit drawing MaryAnn to look up at him, and for the first time, she really saw him in the warm light of the desk lamp. He was indescribably plain, but he did have hair, a lot of it, and it was wavy and dark. His dark hair and dark eyes behind a pair of tortoiseshell glasses seemed too dramatic for him, but he had an unbelievably handsome wide smile. MaryAnn quickly looked back at her tea while they both sat sipping for some minutes until Joe asked her if she wouldn't mind sharing her name.

MaryAnn furrowed her brow. "I'm sorry for being so closed up," she told him. "My name is MaryAnn. My house is down on the gravel road about five blocks from Hill's market. I live in the big old gray house with my mother."

"I know that house," he said. "When I was a kid, the lady that lived there used to throw rocks and yell at me to get lost because she had a little barking dog that followed me along the fence when I rode my bike past. At that age, I think I just wanted to antagonize the owner to see if I could get her to come out and look for rock ammo."

MaryAnn raised an eyebrow. "I think that little dog was Skeeter, and if someone threw rocks at you, that was probably my mother. After a few drinks, she has no patience. When the dog barked, she used to go crazy trying to shut him up."

"But I don't remember ever seeing you there," Joe said.

"I probably wasn't there. My mother shipped me off to live with my grandmother for four years. I didn't come to town until after my gramma died when I was nearly five."

"Ohhh, that makes sense. I was about eight or nine when I'd ride my bike up to the big pond up on the hill and fish, then on the way back, I'd try to get the dog to come out to the fence to reach in and pet him. Sometimes I could, other times no."

MaryAnn chuckled a bit, imagining him running from her mother's rocks. "She has a lousy arm. I doubt she could have hit you," she said after a long sip of tea.

"I know. But she did hit my bike once." They both shared a smile. "So, how are you feeling now? Better with some tea? Did you eat anything today?" Joe was concerned for the girl.

"I don't think I could eat anything. I got some potentially bad news. If my mother finds out, she'll throw a fit and probably throw rocks at me too or simply throw me out of the house."

"You can share it with me. It might make you feel better."

"I don't think that is a very good idea."

"Why not? You are in the house of God. It's not our job to judge. Our job is to help you to overcome your problems."

MaryAnn continued sipping her tea and wondered what this guy's job was anyway? Who is he? His office doesn't look like the maintenance guy, a choir guy, or a hearse-driving guy. Nor does this guy look like the reverend she'd seen shaking hands with patrons on Sunday mornings after the service.

"Is this your office?" she asked.

"Yes. I know it's not very impressive and looks more like a storage closet than an office, but yes, it is my office."

"So you work here?"

"Yes. I'm the associate pastor. I'm kind of in training to be the big guy," he said with a bit of a flourish. "I was a psych major in college and decided the party life wasn't for me. I was dorky and was tired of being picked on for wearing glasses and being quiet, so I looked to the church for comfort and peace. I thought that's what you were doing the other day when we were picking up books."

"Sorry about the books. I hope they are okay. And yes, I hear the organ on Sundays and the church bells and thought I wanted to be part of the church family but was too shy to come alone."

"Too bad you didn't call the office. We could have escorted you and sat with you a few times until you were comfortable."

"Oh, I didn't know about that. I would feel so out of place among the families that come. Sometimes two or three generations were together, and they'd head over to Maxine's Diner for an after-service breakfast buffet. I wish I could have had that. But it wouldn't have worked anyway. A few of the parishioners had kids I knew from school that made it clear over the years that they didn't like me. I'm not pretty and not slim like most of the girls. They look at me like I'm a freak." MaryAnn put her head down looking at the tea in her mug. She felt the sting of tears starting up, so she snapped a tissue from a box on his desk and blew her nose. She giggled a bit at the sound of it in the small office space. "Sorry."

"It's fine," he said, then commented on her troubles of feeling like the school freak, "Well, apparently, we have something in common. I was picked on at school too. The kids would gather at the front vestibule, and I had to walk through them all to go in or out. It was awful."

MaryAnn nodded, "Oh yes, they still do the same thing. I hate leaving school. Before school, if I get there early enough, they haven't crowded at the doorway, but leaving after school, they all hang around yakking, and when I walk up, they all hush and kind of obscure my way out. I have to elbow my way through the wall of silence, yet I hear some whispering and giggling. Some days I'd rather crawl out a window than have to walk through them. I'm sure they are whispering about my weight, or my looks, or my mother." MaryAnn looked at her mug, wishing it had a solution written on it instead of the name of the chapel.

Joe disrupted her momentary thought, "I tell you something, MaryAnn, beauty isn't about your face; it's about what is in your heart and how you treat others. Nobody who is sick, in trouble, or dying cares if you look like a magazine model or a wet dog when you show up to help them. They are simply happy you showed up at all and that someone is caring and helping. That is one of the main reasons I turned to working at the church. People are less to judge my appearance when they need some non-judgmental help. They are almost always thankful for my work."

"You are probably right," MaryAnn sighed, "My mother's work is about her own appearance. She needs to feel above everyone else and beautiful all the time, but no matter how much work she does on herself, she never looks any better to me."

"Beauty comes from within," Joe said. "The more beautiful thoughts you can think and hold in your heart will come through, and others will recognize it. Do you know about Eleanor Roosevelt? She was not a beautiful woman, but she did many things to help people and became a beautiful legacy. Or Mother Theresa, she wasn't exactly a runway model, but the world loved her because of her benevolent giving life."

"Well, maybe that worked for them, but who can I help? Kids at school don't even want to give me a chance. They walk away before I can say hi."

"Maybe that's something we can work on. If you think that's something you'd want to do. That's my job here, helping people."

MaryAnn began to hope his comment was true. He understood the feeling of being shut out by kids at school. Maybe his helping people and his good nature were working because he was beginning to look better every time she glanced up at him. His dark hair was thick and a little wavy, and he wore a neatly trimmed Van-dyke beard that accentuated his beautiful smile. His thick tortoiseshell glasses gave him an authoritative look. MaryAnn shamed herself for looking at Joe as though he was a character in one of her romance novels. She knew she shouldn't think that way. He worked for the church. Besides, she knew she was still a minor and Joe was at least six to eight years older. As she was sipping the last of her tea, she got to smiling thinking about her mother's lousy arm for throwing rocks at Joe.

Joe saw the smile and commented on it. "So the tea is making you feel better?"

She hadn't thought much about feeling better when her thoughts were so involved with Joe's appearance, but now that he mentioned it, yes, she was feeling better. She thanked him for his kindness and concern.

*   *   *

Chapter 10

Sloppy Joe's

Xtra-files

$\mathcal{J}$oe held up the little teapot still warm with its chicken shirt and asked if she'd like a warm-up. She held her mug out and Joe poured the still-steaming tea as she asked if she was keeping him from his work.

Joe looked around at the wreck of papers on his desk and he chuckled, "Does this look like a person that does much paperwork? I realize it looks like I'm very busy, but most of these papers have already been taken care of months ago. They are people's requests for church business, such as asking for prayers, requests for using the church basement for events, copies of marriages and baptisms, just churchy stuff. That big pile on the corner is stuff I have to get re-filed. I hate filing, as you can see."

It was very obvious to MaryAnn that he didn't like filing, not one bit. She knew she was a natural at making things orderly, so she thought about offering to help him after school. He'd been so kind and helpful that she wanted to pay him back for his kindness. She also felt that working in the church would give her a needed spiritual lift, and being around Joe was a bonus. Momentarily she reflected back to the nudge she felt from her menagerie to return to the church. Now it was almost making sense. Was this fate or just dumb luck?

Joe commented on her distant look, "You seem to be someplace else, MaryAnn."

"Oh, well, yes, I was just wondering, could I help you with your filing?" she offered, looking at the pile and not making eye contact with Joe, fearing he'd be ready to say no. She mustered up some courage and took a quick breath, intent on speaking up for a change. When she looked right through his tortoiseshell glasses and into his deep brown eyes, she noticed his lashes so thick and long that they gave his eyes a dewy peaceful look. It made her swallow hard, but she regrouped quickly, knowing she had a small window to make her verbal application. It all came out at once, "I can stop by after school and help. I don't need to get paid. I would be volunteering, and I could spend some time in the church where I don't have to watch my back for my mother's digs. I want to help you since you've been so kind." She held her breath, waiting for the letdown that she assumed was coming, like all the rest of the emotional hits she'd been taking in her life.

Joe thought about her helping for a minute. She was right; she could use getting out and doing something constructive and fulfilling, not to mention he wanted to get rid of that growing stack of letters and documents he was supposed to keep filed. She was also right that working in the church office would feel like a safe zone from school kids and her mother. He didn't take long to answer. "I'll have to run that by the pastor, but I don't see a problem. Do you have a cell phone? I could text you later after I talk to him."

Momentarily exhilarated, then deflated with the cell phone problem, she told him, "No. No texts. My mom won't get me a phone. She said she doesn't want to waste money on someone that has no friends to talk to anyway. She is much happier spending it at the salon or at the Brown Lobster. And I am much happier in my special room away from her wrath when she comes home with a buzz."

Joe was cautiously curious about this young lady that didn't share much about herself, so he leaned back in his chair, clasping his hands behind his head, and calmly said, "A special room? What, like a jail cell?"

MaryAnn was inexplicably comfortable explaining her favorite place in the house to Joe. "No, silly, it's not jail. I call it my special room, but it is actually attic space. My mother won't venture up there as she thinks there are spiders and bats, creepy stuff. I cleaned it up when she's been gone and made myself a safe room."

Joe shook his head at how MaryAnn put herself in sort of an attic jail just to feel safe from her mother's temper. He knew no daughter should fear her mother that way. It started to make sense to him why the young lady was so distrustful. He could see she was a little overweight, not tons, but enough to be different, and teens generally want to fit in, not be different. He considered that the school kids probably picked up on her dredgy self-image and her polluted self-esteem. This girl was suffering her youth away in a secluded attic to avoid any more emotional anguish. He couldn't let it go. "Does your mother ever lock you in?"

"Oh no, it's my choice. I actually like it because I'm alone and don't have to worry about my mom yelling at me."

"So, do you hide away in this special room often?"

"Uh huh. Pretty much every afternoon after school and most evenings after I finish cleaning up supper dishes."

"Isn't that a lot of alone time? Don't you ever get lonely?"

"Well, even though it's part of the attic, it's comforting to me. My mother leaves me alone. She thinks I'm like Cinderella and her mouse friends, but I'm not. I sit and read, and sometimes I cry for my grandmother. She is becoming more and more of a distant memory. My grandmother was so warm and good-hearted, the little that I can remember now. She made me feel safe and loved. I have memories of sitting in her lap, and she'd rock me and quietly sing songs to me. Some were silly, some were churchy, and some were lullabies. My favorites were the Christmas carols, especially "Do You Hear What I Hear." She made me feel good when it was bedtime, and every night it was our special time. She got me a glow-in-the-dark cross, so I'd have a little light when I went to bed. We'd hold it by the lamp while she tucked me in, then she'd turn out the light, and the little cross would glow for me while we said our prayers and until I fell asleep. It seemed so magical.

When I first went to live with my mother after my grandmother died, she'd just tell me to go to bed, and if I didn't hurry up and get in bed, she'd get really angry. After I got in bed, I'd hear ice in a glass and her opening bottles and making a drink. I didn't dare get out of bed. To stay out of her way the rest of the time, I started taking some toys to the attic. Sometimes it was too hot or too cold to play there, but most of the time it was okay and just a relief to be by myself. By the time I was in high school, it was definitely my safe place."

Joe was listening intently, hoping to find some light in her life, but other than her grandmother, she didn't seem to have anything. "Did you ever have a boyfriend? Or sort of a boyfriend? If you are in high school, you should have caught the eye of some young man."

"No. I never look at boys. Not that I'm looking at women either. I just don't want to care about anyone because it hurt me so much when my grandmother was suddenly taken out of my life. Mom didn't tell me for quite a while that Gramma had died. She thought it would be better if I had hope to see her again. Mom would promise that if I was good that we'd go back to visit. So I didn't know about her death until I was in about the third grade. One night mother was drunk, and I dropped a glass in the kitchen, and it broke. She went crazy, yelling and screaming at me while she made me clean it up. During her drunken rant, I was picking up tiny pieces of glass when she viciously told me my gramma was dead and I'd never see her again. I thought I was going to die that night. I wished I would have. I swear my heart exploded in my chest, and my stomach cramped up in knots. It took me weeks and months to get through a day without crying. I never want to hurt like that again. So boys, no. I can walk away. Besides, I can't say that there was ever a guy that took an interest in me."

Joe mulled that over for a minute, "You know, there is someone for everyone in this world if you are open to sharing yourself. How do you know that you'll be hurt again? Maybe some young man could fill your dreams and not leave you."

"I suppose so, but it's always going to be a gamble." MaryAnn's young experience with her family kicked in. "I can't be hurt if I don't get involved. Before my daddy left, he used to gripe at my mother with insults that she wasn't pretty anymore or that she was gaining weight or getting old. So, look at me, how can I think that some boyfriend won't do the same to me eventually? And you can see that I'm not all cute and attractive like most of the girls at school. I've tried to lose weight, but I get upset, and the only thing that seems to settle my stomach is filling it with something."

MaryAnn kept giving Joe puzzles that he found difficult to defend, so he tried a different direction. "That nausea you feel might be medical. Have you seen a doctor about it?"

MaryAnn didn't want to talk about what she'd already heard from the clinic, so she let it slide. "My mother has always told me it's all in my head. What good would a doctor do?"

"Well, it could be something simple. I'm not a doctor, so

I can't diagnose you, but you might be wise to see a doctor about it."

She knew Joe was right and decided to crack the door open a bit to her issues, just leaving out the diagnosis. "I had just come from the clinic when you saw me throwing up. All they did was cause me more stress and anxiety. They weren't helping at all." MaryAnn hung her head remembering what they told her earlier. It set all her guts in motion again but not as severe. Perhaps the tea was helping.

There was silence in the office as the two sat there thinking about the conversation. It was becoming uncomfortable, so Joe said, "If you can wait a few more minutes, I'll go talk to Pastor Bob, and I'll find out if you can volunteer to be my assistant if you are still interested." Joe intentionally mentioned being his assistant to make it sound more important than a simple volunteer to shuffle paper.

"Yes, I can hang for a while. My mom thinks I'm in school. This is her beauty day in town, so she won't be home when the attendance people call to find out why I'm not in school. She still keeps a landline in case some of her old boyfriends call, so the school can't even text her."

Joe winked at her and excused himself from the office. "I'll be back in a couple of minutes."

While he was out, MaryAnn flipped through the stack of papers on his desk and saw baptism information, births, deaths, marriages, and requests for copies of information that occurred at the church decades ago. She didn't know quite how they'd be filed, but she could see that the stack definitely needed some order. She looked at the last paper in the stack. It was dated almost two years ago. She chuckled to herself that, yes, this guy really hated filing.

She didn't see filing cabinets, so she assumed they kept the files somewhere else. Looking around his office, she noticed a bag of chips tucked away in the corner, Carl's Chips. Ahhh, she thought, so he is a closet muncher too. No wonder he understands my feelings so well. Not only is he a muncher, he likes the same chips. As she was studying his desk accouterments, she heard footsteps on the little stairway, and shortly the door squeaked open. Joe was all smiles. "Yes, you can volunteer to be my aide!"

"That's great!" MaryAnn was genuinely happy. "When can I start?"

"Well, Pastor Bob wants you to fill out the usual HR stuff. Just a formality for insurance purposes. And he would like to meet with you first."

MaryAnn clouded over. She really didn't want to meet the gray-haired man she'd seen hand-shaking after Sunday services. Even though he wasn't a huge guy, he seemed like a towering personality.

"Don't worry, MaryAnn. He's a decent man. Whatever happens in his office will never get out. He knows what it's like in a small town."

MaryAnn understood what talk was like in a small town too. Her mother was usually the talk of the town. She couldn't do anything about the talk except try to be a better person, and working at the church just might give her that chance. She also knew if word got out of the clinic about what they thought was wrong with her, there'd be no stopping her mother and the rest of the town from hearing about it, so the church might be her last line of defense. She planned to spend plenty of time praying that the clinic's diagnosis was some kind of ridiculous mistake.

*   *   *

Chapter 11

Pastor-ized

The Interview

*M*aryAnn followed Joe through the hallways of the church, and finally, Joe knocked lightly on the door that said "Pastor." MaryAnn took a deep breath, and Joe heard it. Before he turned the knob, he told her to relax, "Pastor Bob is an okay guy. He's got a lot of life under his belt. He's heard it all." Joe turned the knob and opened the door to the rector's office. It was very spacious compared to Joe's office. Joe's seemed more like a cubby hole in comparison. Joe introduced MaryAnn to Pastor Bob, and they had light handshakes all around causing MaryAnn to blush so hard that she looked sunburned. Then Pastor Bob asked Joe to give them some privacy. Joe smiled at the now panicking MaryAnn. He patted her shoulder as he left, closing the door behind him.

The reverend turned off the background music, then sat in the big leather chair behind his considerable desk, resting his elbows on the arms of the chair and interlocking his fingers not enough to be praying, just enough to seem corporate. "So, young lady, you want to volunteer here?"

MaryAnn nodded in the affirmative.

"Well, what experience do you have?"

MaryAnn froze. Experience? What did he want to hear from her? What could she say...sorting socks for laundry day? Putting groceries away? Sorting her crayons by color? After a silence that went on too long, she finally spoke, knowing the truth would be the best avenue; however the results came down. "I don't have any real experience. I don't know what I can do. All I know is that I'm just lost. I have no friends, and my mother doesn't care if I live or die. The only person who cared about me was my gramma, and she passed before I turned five. I think I'm going to be in big trouble with my mother soon and I have no place to go. I came into your chapel because I needed a safe place to pray where I thought I might be heard. Joe was trying to understand my troubles. He seemed so kind to help me that I wanted to help him in return."

"Are you in love with Joe?"

MaryAnn was shocked and cringed at how blatant his question was, and she was appalled that he would even ask it. She recoiled and said no most emphatically. "I just met him, I was throwing up and he handed me some tissues. He listened to me. Besides, he's much older than me, and I'm not exactly the catch of the century. I'm not all that interested in boys anyway. I like books and the quiet. Joe is so help-oriented that I thought since he helped me, I'd like to help him in return."

Pastor Bob interrupted, "Okay, okay. I hope you understand that I have to ask these tough questions. I can't have young girls coming in here with intentions to flirt with Joe."

MaryAnn felt offended but told him calmly, "I'm not much of a flirt. I don't even know how to flirt." MaryAnn felt the burn of tears coming, so she looked out the window, stung by the reverend's insinuation. Then she wistfully followed up, "I just wanted to help Joe for his kindness today. He obviously doesn't like filing."

Pastor Bob thought about what she said for a few minutes, then shuffled in a file drawer. He pulled out a form and slid it across his desk to her asking if she'd mind filling out as much as she could, explaining that it was church procedure. He slid a pen across the desk and relaxed back in his chair while she slowly picked up the pen and the form looking at what information it required. It was a volunteer application form. She began to fill it out, trying not to make mistakes and using her best penmanship. It was emotionally exhausting doing it while the reverend watched. He was wearing a golf shirt and khakis, so he wasn't dressed in his royal robes, but MaryAnn knew he had them and had earned the right to wear them. She was intimidated by his charismatic presence.

She handed over the form when she'd filled out most of it. He leaned back in his chair again, absorbing the information that she had written. He looked at it far too long, causing MaryAnn to start feeling nervous and start thinking about getting out of there and wanting to stop at the market for a bag of Carl's Chips, then hide in her attic space for the rest of the day. It wasn't even lunch yet.

Pastor Bob cleared his throat, startling MaryAnn's thoughts of chips in the attic. "Well, young lady, I don't see anything that would preclude you from volunteering here. You appear to be in high school. Why are you not in class today?"

"I was sick this morning and went to the clinic. I was throwing up down the block when Joe found me, so he led me here for some hot tea to settle my stomach." MaryAnn looked down at her folded hands, embarrassed having to mention puking on a tree.

"I see," Pastor Bob said. "So, if you are in school on a regular day, when do you think you can volunteer?"

"I can do a few afternoons after school. I don't get a lot

of homework, and when I go home, I tend to snack on stuff until suppertime. I know it's not good, and my mother is always yelling at me about it."

"Your mother does not attend our church, right? Your last name, Jackson, is quite common, but I'm not aware of anyone in town with that last name."

"I told Joe when I was born, my mother dumped me at my grandmother's. Gramma died before I turned five, and my mom was furious that she was then stuck with having a little kid to tend to. She made it clear she did not want to be a mother, and apparently, she didn't want to be a wife either. My parents fought all the time, and my dad, Bud Jackson, finally left. I don't know where he went. When the divorce was final, mom took her maiden name back but left me with my dad's last name."

"Who is your mother?"

"Rita. Rita Blackmost."

"Ohhhh, oooookay....Blackmost. Yes, I've heard of her. She spends a lot of time in my sister-in-law's salon, the Hair Pin Curves."

"That's right, the Hair Pin Curves. She also spends a lot of time sitting at the Brown Lobster and Jerry's Gin Joint. Kind of like it's her part-time job.

"I wasn't going to mention that in case you weren't familiar."

"I'm very familiar. I've become her maid. She gets home from the Brown Lobster a little tipsy, and I'd better have dinner ready for her. Then after supper, she'll wait until I get the kitchen cleaned up and go to my room, then I hear her fixing another drink. Some mornings she's passed out on the sofa and never made it to bed. I'll be eighteen in a few months, and I hope to be able to get a job and move away from her. She's never been much of a

mother. I'd have been better off in an orphanage."
MaryAnn noticed that, in a strange way, it felt good to
unload to this higher spiritual being. She felt better,
having blurted out her frustrations.

"I know it's hard," Pastor Bob said, "but you have to
understand that if your mother is drinking a lot, she is not
thinking straight. Even if she hasn't had a drink in a day or
so, it still affects her mood and outlook. Has she ever had
a job?"

"No, sir. She got some money when my grandma died
and got the house when she divorced my dad. She gets a
check from my dad now and then. That was supposed to
carry us through. I think it was supposed to be child
support money, but I can tell it's booze support. I don't
know how she gets all the money for her salons, spas, and
other stuff. She goes to the bank a lot. Maybe she is
figuring out a way to rob it. I babysit sometimes and help
a couple of the old people around our neighborhood to
earn a little for myself, but how she gets money, I don't
know."

"So, with your babysitting, you are getting out other
than school?"

"Yes, sir, a little."

"Very well, MaryAnn. Welcome to our church. And you
are right, Joe can use help with his filing. We'll help you
too. We'll help you find your guardian angels."

MaryAnn started to cry. Help. That's all she really
wanted to hear from somebody.

*   *   *

Chapter 12

Hanging with Joe

Exposing the Desktop

So now you know how MaryAnn became a church volunteer, but she only worked with Joe. MaryAnn went to the church after school, and to make sure none of the kids saw her going there, she and Joe had a system in place for MaryAnn to go to the back of the church, and Joe would let her in through the service entrance that was obscured by some landscaping. Most days, MaryAnn spent her time organizing and filing documents and was given access to the church basement archive files. As the days passed, she was learning a lot about the town's people, including a few secrets, but Joe told her that she must keep the secrets to herself and never share the information with anyone. MaryAnn wondered who she would tell anyway.

Some afternoons when the paperwork was caught up, MaryAnn would sit and read in Joe's office while he was out helping some of the congregants through their troubles. Other times, when she was caught up with filing, she and Joe would sip tea and talk. Joe learned a lot about MaryAnn's life, but he knew she was still hiding something. When he'd ask her certain things, he knew the body language signs of avoiding answers. But on other topics, she conversed well as they talked about books and favorite movies. Sometimes Joe would pray with her. On occasion, they'd share some snacks while working on sorting paperwork.

MaryAnn became comfortable talking to Joe during the weeks of her volunteer work, and they were becoming friends despite the age difference. MaryAnn seemed to be an older soul anyway, and Joe still had a bit of childish mischief in him as he'd tease MaryAnn good-naturedly just to make her laugh. He saw that MaryAnn was not particularly pretty, but when she smiled, it improved her looks and attitude immensely, and he wanted her to capitalize on that. Joe also noticed she'd gained a bit of weight recently and was concerned, but he wasn't going to point out what she probably already knew. In his studies of psychology, he knew when people were putting on weight, they were always aware of it. He also knew that over-eating was giving them momentary comfort in a complicated emotional period of their lives or was helping them deal with overwhelming depression. Joe wanted to help her past all that. He wondered if things were deteriorating between her and her mother, causing the additional weight. Still, he had to wait until she addressed the problem.

Meanwhile, MaryAnn was making a few bucks babysitting an aging old man so his aide could take a break. She used the cash to buy an extra package of Razzies as a treat for Joe. She made the tea for him too. They enjoyed the cakes and tea, chuckling about having to lick their sticky fingers like toddlers until Joe went to the restroom for some paper towels.

So, as you can tell, MaryAnn was enjoying her volunteer work. She also enjoyed Joe's friendship and finally got his desk cleared off so he could see the top of it. One afternoon, he brought in a pizza to share with MaryAnn to celebrate his desktop appearance since now he had a surface to set the box on. It was all working out well for both of them.

Then one day, after a couple of months of routine,

MaryAnn didn't show up to file. Without her having a cell phone, Joe couldn't contact her to find out what had happened. She missed the next time as well. When she didn't show up a third time, Joe hung out in the town square when the kids got out of school to see if he could see her, but she wasn't there. He considered stopping by the old gray house on the edge of town, but he wasn't interested in getting mixed up with MaryAnn's mother. He was becoming very concerned. Could her mother have done something unthinkable to MaryAnn?

*   *   *

Chapter 13

Walking and Wishing

Star Light, Star Bright

What Joe didn't know was that over a week ago, MaryAnn's mother had a drunken meltdown at the Brown Lobster, and Benny the bartender finally threw her out. She teetered down to Jerry's Gin Joint, but they wouldn't serve her either, resulting in Rita throwing a nasty public tantrum. She wanted another drink. As the booze buzz waned, she became disruptive and louder, stumbling in the streets and cussing at people that were looking at her. She showed up at home in a semi-drunken fury; angry at the town, angry at the people, angry at her life. As she hunted out her booze stash around the house, she started throwing things and swearing loudly, nearly knocking pictures off the walls. She only stopped ranting when she stopped to fix herself another drink, then she'd fire up again.

MaryAnn came down to see what the racket was, and her mother slung a plate at her catching MaryAnn in the forehead. It was a minor cut, but it bled badly. When Rita sobered up a little, she tried to apologize to MaryAnn but blamed MaryAnn for being in the way of the plate. She also blamed MaryAnn for her drinking, telling MaryAnn that she hated coming home to see her face. Then Rita fixed herself another drink.

MaryAnn had enough. She was tempted to tell her mother what the clinic told her about her belly nausea. She knew it would be like tossing a grenade at her mother. But she knew it could cause her mother to get blind drunk and possibly wander the town ranting about her daughter's condition. So instead, MaryAnn waited until her mother passed out on the sofa.

At first, MaryAnn considered calling her Aunt to come to get her but using the house phone in the kitchen was dangerous. Her mother could easily hear everything from her throne on the sofa and would be atomically angry if she heard MaryAnn calling Aunt Rachel. So MaryAnn decided she'd sneak out and make the twelve or so-mile journey on foot. She stuffed a few things into a grocery bag and left. She knew it was a long way to her Aunt Rachel's, but Aunt Rachel was more like her grandmother; kind, understanding, and wasn't a drunk. Aunt Rachel would know what to do.

The gravel and dirt roads out of town were hard to walk on, and it was getting dark, but MaryAnn steeled herself with the anger she'd built toward her mother over the years and started walking.

As night settled in, she'd been walking quite a while when the moon began to rise. A few pick-up trucks passed her, kicking up the dust, but nobody stopped to offer her a ride. As she walked and her anger cooled, she became concerned about walking at night with the movement of foxes, coyotes, and an occasional bobcat, but the autumn moon was full, the air was clear, and the night sky was full of twinkling stars. It was easy to see if anything was on the road that might present a problem.

She looked up to the stars a few times along the way, wondering if her grandmother was watching over her. Her grandmother had spoken of the stars many times and taught MaryAnn how to wish on a star. So tonight, more than any other night, it seemed appropriate to wish on a star. She picked out an exceptionally bright one and concentrated on it.

"Star light, Star bright
Brightest star I see tonight,
I wish I may, I wish I might,
Have this wish, I wish tonight."

Then she shouted up to the star, asking for the same thing she always asked for in her prayers; a friend, someone to love, and someone to love her. She noticed that wishing on a star seemed similar to praying but enjoyably louder. She hoped the star she picked out heard her, and if that one didn't, she hoped one of the rest of them did.

There were no places to stop on the rural roads, just a few farmhouses way back off the gravel. There was no chance of getting a drink or asking for a rest, especially in the wee hours of the night. And walking on the gravel road was slow and difficult, especially when the moon began to wane and it became hard to see.

It was near dawn when she finally turned down Aunt Rachel's road, stumbling toward the farmhouse. MaryAnn was exhausted, her feet hurt, and she couldn't decide which was worse, her feet aching or her dry throat.

It was then she saw the headlights of a pick-up truck heading toward her, so she hid her face as the truck whizzed by, but seconds later, she heard the truck skid on the gravel, stop, and start to back up.

MaryAnn kept walking and picked up her pace. She knew guys in trucks liked to stop and harass lone girls on the road. It was barely dawn, and likely they were out drinking all night. She gritted her teeth waiting for the inevitable as the truck began to pace her in reverse. Then she heard a power window roll down and cringed at what she expected to hear next and braced herself for it.

Then she heard, "MaryAnn? Is that you?" in a kindly

female voice.

MaryAnn jerked her head around and saw it was Aunt Rachel driving the truck. The relief MaryAnn felt caused her to break into tears.

"Oh my God, girl, get in the truck." Aunt Rachel told her.

MaryAnn got in the truck wiping tears, dirt, and road dust off her face while her Aunt handed her some fresh tissues.

"Don't tell me you walked all the way from home. What happened? You could have called me. I'd have come to get you."

"Mom is drinking heavier than ever. She threw stuff at me. Told me I was too ugly to look at. I can't take it anymore, Aunt Rae." MaryAnn broke down in deep sobbing breaths.

Aunt Rachel put the truck in park and scooted over in the seat to grab MaryAnn up in her arms and hold her tight. Aunt Rachel noticed the cut on MaryAnn's head and knew she could call the police on her sister, but that would only bring more drama down on MaryAnn. Instead, Aunt Rachel told Mary Ann she was going to take her back to her farm and fix her head, then fix her some breakfast. MaryAnn cried more. Someone was actually going to take care of her and even better, cook for her.

*　　*　　*

Chapter 14

Farm House Secrets

And Squeaky Floors

They spent the morning sharing news and cooking duties, making a huge breakfast with bacon, hash browns, toast, and eggs; MaryAnn's favorite meal. Aunt Rachel told MaryAnn about her vineyard that had a good year in grapes, and the orchards did well too. She sold the grapes for a good price to a local winery and was also able to sell most of the orchard crop. She got enough money from the sales that she was able to buy a newer truck and a few other things she wanted and still put some money in the bank. MaryAnn told Aunt Rachel about her volunteer work at the church and her mother's increasing binge drinking and chronic attempts at preserving her youth. They talked and talked all through breakfast and cleaning up.

Aunt Rachel could see that MaryAnn looked exhausted from the walk, the stress, and everything else.

"You should stay here for a few days for things to calm down. I'll call your mom and tell her where you are, and I'll call the school.

"I should be getting back home, though," MaryAnn told her. "Mom will just be madder if no one is cooking or cleaning. And I feel bad bumming food off you."

"Don't you worry about food. I have plenty, and my freezer is darn near full for winter. It's nice for me to have a little company like this on occasion. Sometimes I wish I'd have had kids, but this is the life I made for myself. Me, my farm, my grapes."

Aunt Rachel led MaryAnn upstairs to the spare room picking out some clean bedding from the linen closet along the way. MaryAnn always loved the way her bedding smelled so fresh from hanging it outdoors to dry.

While fluffing pillows and unfolding a couple of quilts on the bed, Aunt Rachel told MaryAnn that she should take a shower, then rest for a bit, and they would talk more later. She was heading into town for some supplies when she saw MaryAnn on the road, and she still needed to get those errands done. The weather was predicting a storm at the end of the week, and she didn't want to be caught without some necessities.

MaryAnn soon heard the truck start up and crunch down the gravel driveway. It was so peaceful and quiet in the old farmhouse except for a few creaks now and then. There were no worries about her mother coming in and ranting about something.

MaryAnn took her time, enjoying the luxury of not having to hurry. She savored the long hot shower washing the road grit off with one of the sweet-scented soaps Aunt Rachel left on the counter. After the shower, she brushed the wet knots out of her hair as she watched herself in the mirror. She was always disappointed when she saw that she wasn't pretty. She stood sideways and looked to see if she had a protruding belly, and so far, it was merely something she could call a Carl's Chips gut.

She put on the clean sweat suit Aunt Rachel laid out, then stretched out on the comfy bed, wondering if she should explain her possible "condition" to her Aunt and what her Aunt might say about that. Would Aunt Rachel throw her out too?

MaryAnn dozed off while trying not to worry about the choices she would have to make very soon.

* * *

Chapter 15

Invitation

Autumn Falls

*M*aryAnn woke to the smell of something wonderful cooking. As she rubbed her eyes, she could see by the dimming light that it was late afternoon. She felt foolish to have slept most of the day away, but it was a peaceful good sleep.

"Hi there, nightingale," Aunt Rachel said as MaryAnn stepped into the kitchen. "Did you have a good nap?"

MaryAnn yawned, "Yes, ma'am. I must have slept really well. When I woke, I wasn't sure where I was for a few seconds. Mmmm, whatever you are cooking, it smells great."

"Hope you brought your appetite. I'm fixing us some supper; pork chops and some mashed potatoes. I haven't fixed a big dinner for a long time as there's not much of a reason to cook for myself. I got some rolls ready for the oven, and I'm steaming some string beans too. A good dinner....for two."

"You don't need to do all this for me. I should be getting back home. Mom will be worried and call the cops or something if nobody is fixing supper for her."

"Your mother does not need a maid. She's perfectly capable to fix herself a meal. I called her and left a message this morning that you came to my house, but she hasn't responded yet. She doesn't seem to be too worried."

"That's my mother for you," MaryAnn sighed.

After supper, while they were finishing the dishes, Aunt Rachel was wiping her hands on the dishtowel when she told MaryAnn she could stay with her as long as she needed. MaryAnn thanked her over and over but knew she didn't want Aunt Rachel to get the vindictive chewing she knew her mother was capable of, especially if she'd been drinking. She also knew she couldn't stay with her Aunt forever, even if it was safe, welcoming, and comfortable. She knew she'd have to leave, but how and when?

So as it happened, MaryAnn stayed with Aunt Rachel as a few days melted into a few weeks while the last cool days of summer turned to autumn. Fall stole away the summer greens leaving behind the deep earth tones of reds, browns, and golds until the leaves let go of their birthplaces to enjoy the brief floating freedom from the branches on which they were born. The North wind ruffled them down the road like thousands of tiny ballerinas rushing to the stage for their last performance. The air became crisp and chilled, mildly scented with the woodsy fragrance of distant burning oak leaves, and daylight closed her eyes earlier every day.

As the days continued to pass, they only heard from Rita when she was drunk, and Aunt Rachel simply hung up on her. MaryAnn was eating healthier as there were no markets nearby to pick up snacks. Besides, Aunt Rachel enjoyed cooking for her, and sometimes MaryAnn would cook for Aunt Rachel. There wasn't much to do with the grapes at this time of year, so Aunt Rachel had a lot of personal time to sit and talk. MaryAnn noticed that she no longer felt like puking all the time and attributed that to her Aunt's calm, accepting demeanor and eating sensibly.

Although she felt like she was losing a few pounds, her belly appeared to have a significant bulge which kept MaryAnn wondering, was the clinic right or wrong?

As the weeks passed, MaryAnn's condition became obvious. She kept pulling her sweatshirt down over her belly to try to minimize the pooch hoping Aunt Rachel didn't notice, but in fact, Aunt Rachel did notice. She couldn't help but notice. MaryAnn's "beer gut" was definitely emerging. Even though she saw that MaryAnn's face was thinning a bit, her gut was having the opposite problem.

Aunt Rachel was not naive. She knew sometimes teenage boys liked to coerce unpopular girls to get them to do what they wanted. She knew it from her own personal experience having had her own nightmare to live with. Aunt Rachel could see that MaryAnn wasn't someone most boys would be interested in other than as a pubescent conquest from exploding hormones and chalking it up for bragging rights. Could her own niece have been used by a shifty punk somehow without even knowing it? If that growing belly was evidence, there were only two possibilities; a huge tumor or something else. She had to figure out a way to get MaryAnn to talk about it, just to be sure.

Aunt Rachel didn't want to add to MaryAnn's stress by pressing for details. She knew MaryAnn already had plenty of issues with her mother, not only the drinking but MaryAnn's disappointment that her own mother didn't care enough to call or check on her unless she was drunk. So Aunt Rachel put having "the talk" on the back burner as the holidays approached.

*   *   *

Chapter 16

Telling Tales

What Child Was This?

*A*fter a quiet Thanksgiving, MaryAnn helped Aunt Rachel prepare for the Christmas holiday. Aunt Rachel usually didn't do a lot of holiday things, but they did bake cookies together and hung a few of the old strands of lights around the front porch railing. Very few folks drove down the dirt road after dark, but it was still nice to see the pretty lighted colors out of the front window against all the dark greys and browns of the surrounding rural landscape of winter. Aunt Rachel came home one day with a small live Christmas tree saying she'd plant it after the holiday and that she had a good place for a Christmas tree to grow on her farm. MaryAnn knew Aunt Rachel had a place in her heart for all living things.

One evening, while Aunt Rachel was knitting and MaryAnn was stoking the fireplace, the two were chatting. Aunt Rachel was telling stories about what the holidays were like when she and MaryAnn's mother were kids. Then out of the blue, MaryAnn asked Aunt Rachel why she never had children.

Aunt Rachel was silent for a few minutes as she thought back to the time of her life when all things were still possible. She put her knitting down, looked at the lighted Christmas tree, and simply said she had a child.

MaryAnn looked stunned.

"Oh yes," Aunt Rachel said, "I did, many, many years ago. The story is long, and the reasons don't matter, but yes, I had a little girl. The young man I was so in love with, I'd have done anything to keep him. I thought I'd work my womanly ways on him and that it would kindle his desire for me, and his love would burn so hot that he'd never leave me." Aunt Rachel made a face. "But pffft....as soon as I gave myself to him, he was gone. That ONE time, the one time I let my guard down, he took what he wanted of me and bailed. I felt empty afterward, there was no love in him, and deep down I knew it, but for some reason I still wanted him. He shunned me at school, of course, but when he could get me alone, he would try to get me to sleep with him again.

At least I had half a brain and kept making excuses to be busy, even though my heart still wanted him." Aunt Rachel scowled as she looked out the window at the bare winter branches. "I was apparently struck stupid, or blind, or both!" Aunt Rachel signed heavily and was silent for a minute before continuing. "I think all young girls have dreams of a school crush that lasts forever. I sure thought after sleeping with him that one time it would mean we would be paired forever with some magical superglue. I didn't understand that he simply wanted to use me, then brag about it at school. It was an awful time. So not only was I used, I was also unceremoniously dumped. I wanted to die of a broken heart over here and outrage at his lies over there. And, of course, the rumor mill at school was worse. I wanted to retaliate, but your grandma told me not to. It would just incite more trouble for me. Besides, I thought I still loved him! It is amazing how stupid we are when we are young and feel that first love for someone. Then it is not reciprocated." Aunt Rachel sipped her evening tea and picked up her knitting.

"What happened, if you don't mind me asking?" MaryAnn said while still holding the log intended for the fireplace.

"I think you are old enough to know now. As you can guess, I panicked. I tried to hide it like young girls do. I've forgotten how far along I was when your grandmother noticed it. Back then, it was uncommon and totally unacceptable to be a pregnant teenager. Your grandmother found a place that helped young unmarried women get through the situation. I stayed there for the last two months of the pregnancy. The people there were nice and understanding, and through the course of those weeks tried to make me feel good about myself. They were convincing me that I didn't do anything wrong. They made it sound like it was fate or something, and my most important job, as they told me, was ...." Aunt Rachel stopped momentarily as a few tears appeared. "....was for me to produce a healthy infant for a childless couple to adopt."

MaryAnn dropped the log. She was stunned for a minute, then jumped up and knelt at Aunt Rachel's feet, patting her knee, trying to comfort her obvious sudden distress at her story. "It's okay, Aunt Rae. You don't have to share your story. It is apparently painful. You don't have to go through it on my account."

Aunt Rachel grabbed a tissue, blew her nose, and dabbed a few tears away. "Oh, I have to tell you the rest of this. You need to know," she said, composing herself enough to finish her story.

"When I first arrived at the home with all the other girls there, the atmosphere was almost electric. There was always much excitement about our having babies. But they didn't tell us they were grooming us to give up our newborns for adoption. We found out later that childless couples were willing to pay big bucks to the home, paying all our expenses in exchange for a newborn from a healthy young teenager. They groomed me for weeks to give up my baby as the right thing to do. As it happened, I only saw her for a few minutes after she was born, and they swept her away. All I knew was the papers I signed meant I could never know where she went. At first, I was relieved, but as days passed, I realized that was not a decision I would have made had I not been brainwashed for weeks. Once I gave that baby up, they were in a rush to get me out of the place. That's when your grandmother and I realized that as soon as one of the girls had her baby, she was separated from it. Then she was rushed to sign papers and was sent home as quickly as possible so she couldn't change her mind or be able to tell the other girls what was going on. There was no choice. It was pure and simple brainwashing. Your grandmother would have welcomed an infant in the house, just like she welcomed you when Rita had you a few years later."

"I'm so sorry, Aunt Rae," MaryAnn said, holding back tears thinking how Aunt Rachel had kept that in her heart for so long.

Aunt Rachel continued, "It was a few years after that I met Race. I was never overly crazy about him, but he loved me. I felt I had been used by the first guy and hurt beyond measure. At least if I wasn't crazy in love with Race, he couldn't hurt me when he was done using me. But he apparently loved me a lot. We got married. I never told him of the child. Race didn't want kids anyway. He wanted the vineyard. He was good at it and worked hard for years. But then the cancer got him. I've been happily alone since. I've thought a lot about my baby girl, and I tried to track her down, but court records are sealed, and they closed down that girls' home years ago. So I'll never know what happened to her. She'd be about ten years older than you now. She's your cousin. Your mom was real little when that was happening. Your gramma told your mom that I was away at camp, so she doesn't know either."

Aunt Rachel felt this was now the time to address MaryAnn's condition, so she kept going. "But I'm telling you this story now because it sure looks to me like you are getting exceptionally round in your belly the past couple of weeks. Whatever you choose to do is your business, and I won't interfere, but at least tell me if you loved the guy."

MaryAnn was stunned for a few minutes, but after the shock wore off, she realized she'd have to come clean as Aunt Rachel wasn't going to let it go, and it seemed like she'd understand. So MaryAnn began the story and told Aunt Rachel about going to the clinic and what their test results said and explained that there was no boy, not a loved boy, not any boy, ever, and that she thought the test results were incorrect or someone else's samples until a few months ago. MaryAnn became tearful, knowing how ridiculous and impossible it all sounded.

"You know," Aunt Rachel said, "it could be something like a false pregnancy. I've heard it can mimic a pregnancy pretty well, especially in stressful situations. Are you sure it's not this guy at the church? With you going there every couple of days, are you sure he didn't take advantage of you?"

MaryAnn started crying, trying to explain that she was positive there was no guy. "The guy at the church doesn't know anything about it either. He is a friend, plain and simple. There is nothing more between us."

"Perhaps it's your mind blanking it out. If you were violated, maybe your brain is blocking a very unpleasant situation."

"I don't think so," MaryAnn said. "I think I'd know. I'm sure I'd remember that."

Aunt Rachel tried to lighten the conversation, "The first time, yes, you'd remember it. I don't think I'll ever forget that myself." But MaryAnn didn't seem amused, just frightened.

"Well, I'm sure there's a logical explanation for this.

Let's try not to overthink it right now. Perhaps after the holiday, I can take you to my doctor, and we'll see what is happening."

MaryAnn didn't want to do a doctor visit, but maybe Aunt Rachel was right. Perhaps it was a mix-up at the clinic or a false pregnancy. At least Aunt Rachel's doctors were in the county seat and not near her mother or her school.

After she went to bed, she felt a little movement in her Carl's Chips gut and realized that this was no false pregnancy, mistake, or weird case of gas. MaryAnn couldn't sleep. She tossed and turned and would have paced the floors, but the floorboards squeaked too much, and she didn't want to disturb Aunt Rachel. She realized then that she'd have to leave. She didn't want Aunt Rachel to get in trouble for hiding her, and she didn't want Aunt Rachel to have to suffer all the memories of her lost little one. She called Joe early the next morning on Aunt Rachel's phone.

"I can't talk long, I can't explain much, but I need a ride out of town. Can you come get me and take me to the city?" MaryAnn rattled at Joe.

Joe was curious about what was going on and why MaryAnn had disappeared from her volunteer position for the past couple of months, but he was glad to know she was okay. He never did try to get in touch with MaryAnn's mother, as he simply didn't want to be on the back end of her shovel. He had hoped MaryAnn would show up eventually. So now that she contacted him out of the blue to help her get out of town, he asked himself if he should help her again or should he tell Reverend Bob first.

While Joe's mind was spinning with questions and getting no details from MaryAnn, the two worked out a simple get-away plan. The following Tuesday evening, he'd pick her up at Aunt Rachel's and take her to the city almost 100 miles away. It would be Christmas Eve, and everyone in town would be busy with their families and wouldn't notice them leaving. Joe prayed his car would make it, and if it did, he would know he was doing the right thing. He'd easily be back before Christmas morning services, so he wouldn't be missed.

*   *   *

Chapter 17

Pick Up Lines

Hit the Road, Joe

And now, dear reader, you understand why MaryAnn is standing in the cold and snow in front of Aunt Rachel's farmhouse, waiting for Joe's car to come down the dirt road to take her to freedom.

The snow had accumulated slowly to about three or four inches, nothing dramatic, just blustery winter dust, but the wind was freezing, and her cheeks were feeling chapped. She left a note for Aunt Rachel knowing she would find it in the morning. She was going to borrow Aunt Rachel's cell phone but knew it was traceable and knew that without a cell phone, no one could track her. But she also had no way to call Joe and find out where he was. He said he'd pick her up at ten. It was now almost ten-fifteen. She had a plastic grocery sack of her things clutched to her chest to block the snow from going down her shirt, but the crunched-up bag was accumulating snow too.

Finally, she saw a lone headlight in the distance, yes, only one light, the other burned out months ago. Joe had been dodging cops to avoid getting a ticket when he had to drive at night. Usually, he made a point to do his errands during the day when it didn't matter if he had one, two, or no headlights. His pay didn't allow for much of anything extra, so it would be a few more weeks before he could get his headlight fixed. Joe managed his life on his meager funds, and sometimes a few generous folks helped him out. Joe bent over backward with appreciation, always promising he'd pay it back or pay it forward. Folks in town liked him. He was a warm, trusting guy and always made time to listen to their problems. And now he felt it was part of his job to help MaryAnn and get her to the city. She sounded desperate over the phone, so he felt he had to try to help her out. As he neared Aunt Rachel's, he saw MaryAnn's now portly silhouette on the sidewalk in front of the vintage Christmas lights strung on the railing of Aunt Rachel's front porch. Had he known MaryAnn would be standing outside waiting in the cold, he would have rushed over sooner. Why would she be standing out in the cold and not inside waiting?

Joe pulled up, leaned over the passenger seat, and ratcheted the door handle around to get the door open. When MaryAnn grabbed the door and yanked it open wide, Joe got a glimpse of her shape under the misfit coat. She had obviously gained a lot of weight. He sat there in shock as she tossed her plastic bag in the back, plunked into the passenger seat, and pulled the door shut, "Let's go! Let's go!" she whispered to him. "Let's get out of here before Aunt Rachel sees me. She'll try to make me stay."

Joe looked at her for a brief incredulous second but saw the stress on MaryAnn's face, so he dutifully put the car in gear and drove slowly away, the tires crunching in the snow and gravel on the road as they left the safety of Aunt Rachel's home. He did not ask MaryAnn any questions and knew nothing of her urgent need to leave.

As they drove in silence, Joe kept glancing at MaryAnn. She looked tired for her young years. Whatever the secret was that she was keeping was obviously wearing on her. He wanted to talk about her plans, but he knew when it was time for her to talk that she would be the one to start it.

Finally, after a few minutes, MaryAnn did speak. Her voice was soft, "You got a radio in here for some music?" Joe fiddled with the radio and punched station buttons until he got instrumental holiday music and turned the volume down.

The ride across the backroads was bumpy. MaryAnn held her belly in her hands, trying to avoid bouncing around. Joe was aware that her beer gut was considerably larger than the last time he had seen her, but he considered she was a little on the chubby side anyway, so maybe it was nothing but nervous eating. Even so, his concern was growing about her welfare. If she was still underage and he was an adult, he wondered just how much trouble her mother would cause him if she wanted to rat him out. Even worse, how much trouble her mother might cause the church if he was caught helping MaryAnn out of town. He didn't even know where he was helping her escape to or why, but he was pretty sure it wasn't to go Christmas shopping.

*   *   *

Chapter 18

Bumpy Roads

Ticket to Ride!

They bumped along the barren county roads until
they neared the town, then turned on various
streets and back alleys to make sure they didn't go
anywhere near MaryAnn's mother's house. Joe also drove
as far away from people and the church as possible as he
aimed for the state highway south of town.

Both sat in silence, staring ahead until they got to the
highway ramp. Joe stopped and turned to MaryAnn. "Are
you sure you want to do this?" She nodded. She was sure.
Joe thought he saw the trail of a tear on her cheek, but he
was getting onto the highway and didn't want to ask. His
mind was already going faster than his car wondering
what on earth her plan was.

The two-lane state road was nearly empty of traffic, so
driving wasn't a problem, even with snow collecting here
and there. But it wasn't long before a pair of headlights
popped up behind them. Joe didn't think anything odd of it
until he noticed it had gained on him until the vehicle was
right behind him. The state road was long and flat with
plenty of dotted lines for passing, so Joe wasn't worried.
He deliberately drove slightly under the speed limit
knowing his tailpipe blew a little smoke when he stepped
on the accelerator, so he would simply nurse it until the

vehicle passed. But the vehicle didn't pass. It followed them for about a mile or two. Then suddenly, they heard its siren and saw the flashing police lights.

"Oh no!" Joe said. They both were shocked at being pulled over by the sheriff. MaryAnn ducked her face down, and Joe stared straight ahead as the patrol car pulled behind them and parked. MaryAnn started worrying that Aunt Rachel or her mother might have called in a run-away or missing person report. Joe worried that Rita might have called to have him arrested. They both knew they were only gone for about forty-five minutes. How could MaryAnn be considered "missing" in less than an hour?

Joe dug out his driver's license and was tapping it nervously on the steering wheel as the officer approached their vehicle. Joe rolled his window down even before the officer asked.

"Sorry, officer. My speedometer must not be working. I thought I was about seven miles an hour under the speed limit."

The officer tilted his hat back on his head. "I didn't pull you over for speeding, young man. I pulled you over to tell you they are talking about closing the road ahead soon because the wind is blowing snow drifts onto the roadway closer to the city. Are you headed home or heading out?" The officer looked in the car with his flashlight and saw a very pregnant young lady.

MaryAnn was freaking out that the officer might ask her for her identification. She had nothing other than a library card. Her mother wouldn't let her drive, so she had no driver's license. Joe was sweating that someone had called in about him picking up MaryAnn. He tried to be as affable as possible with the officer, unbuttoning his coat at the top, hoping his clerical collar could be seen.

"No, sir. We were, uh, making a run to Walmart in the

city to pick up a few gifts we forgot to get. It's the only thing open this late on Christmas Eve. We were hoping to get back home before the weather got too awful. Is it much worse in the city?"

"It's getting bad. I hope they don't close it before you can get back home." The officer clicked off his flashlight. "Be careful, Reverend. Your wife there looks like she doesn't need to get stuck someplace off the road."

"Yes, sir. Thank you, Officer. Have a Merry Christmas, sir."

Joe rolled up his window as he watched the officer in the rearview get back to his vehicle, then exhaled enough air to fill the Astrodome. But his relief didn't last long. "I gotta move now!" he told MaryAnn. "If he gets in front of us, he'll see I don't have a headlight, and he'll pull us over again and ticket me, maybe haul me in. If he figures out you aren't really a wife and you're just a teenager, my life will be over!"

MaryAnn was too busy doing her own fretting to do much of anything constructive. She hadn't even told Joe the pregnancy story yet, although she figured that he'd already figured that out, figuratively.

"Ok," Joe said, well aware that he had an underage girl in his car. "I saw a side road off the highway back a mile or so. I'm going to make a U-turn and go back to it to get off the highway for a bit, so the sheriff doesn't see my busted headlight." Joe didn't see any traffic around, and while the officer was situating himself in his car, Joe goosed his accelerator to get back on the road making his engine cough a bit and blow a cloud of smoke out the tailpipe, and he began to look where he'd pull his U-turn on the highway.

"Are you insane?" MaryAnn asked.

"No. I figure if the sheriff can't see my headlight when I

make the turn, he won't know I only have one. By the time my exhaust smoke clears in this snow, he'll see we turned around. Maybe he'll think we went back home. He'll only see my tail lights after I make the turn. We can't chance getting stopped again. You are underage, and neither of us wants to be hauled into the sheriff's office."

"How do you know all your tail lights work?" she asked.

"He'd have said something when he pulled us over." Joe was now nudging his car toward the center lane getting ready to make his move.

"I don't think this is going to work," MaryAnn said

Joe was quietly mumbling a prayer, then told MaryAnn to hang on. "I sure hope this is legal!" MaryAnn hung onto her belly as Joe smashed on the accelerator to belch out his shroud of secrecy from the tailpipe. Then he cranked the steering wheel a hard left directing his car across the highway. The car wheeled around to the opposite lane as he headed back the other way. The sheriff's car was now only visible in his rearview heading toward the city. "Now I gotta find that road and get off the highway for a few minutes."

"Jeez, Joe," MaryAnn said quietly, "I'm starting to feel like I'm in a crime movie."

Joe flicked on his lone bright that wasn't very bright. "Keep your eyes open for that side road," he said as he watched in his rearview to see if the sheriff might have seen his lonely headlight in the U-turn. Thankfully, the sheriff kept going. "Whew!" Joe exhaled. "That's a relief."

"Maybe he's got bigger fish to fry tonight with the storm and all," MaryAnn said.

"Or maybe he's calling it in and asking for backup. Where's that damn road!" Joe winced that he swore in front of MaryAnn. His lone headlight didn't make the search for a small gravel road in the dark any easier, especially in the falling flurries.

Suddenly MaryAnn pointed ahead. "There! I think that's the road there!"

"Good eye, MaryAnn. I think that's it!" Joe slowed the car as he approached the side road, then quickly turned onto the dark gravel. He was still going at a pretty good clip causing quite a bit of bouncing around on the rocks and frozen ruts.

MaryAnn looked back for as long as she could see through the trees and weeds, watching the sheriff's tail lights fade out of view. "I think we'll be okay now. The sheriff never turned around. Maybe we can slow down a bit now." She settled back in her seat clutching her full belly in both hands, thankful to have avoided any additional drama.

*   *   *

Chapter 19

Lost in Snow Where

Two for the Road

The twisting dirt and gravel road was so poorly maintained that Joe wondered if it was somebody's driveway. Then after a mile or so, they came to a crossroad and decided to take the crossroad, thinking they would wind up heading back toward the highway. Joe worried about the accumulating snow as his tires were nearly bald and were slipping a bit now and then. And he still didn't know why MaryAnn wanted to get to the city. He assumed it had something to do with her mother.

Joe squinted to see through the slushy windshield as they bumped and slid along, wishing he'd have replaced the wiper blades before winter hit. After they had been driving awhile, nothing looked familiar, and he had no idea where he was. He was hoping MaryAnn didn't notice. He knew if they'd have stayed on the highway to the interstate, they'd have made it to the city by now. Joe was feeling confused about directions and was also confused about what MaryAnn's plans were. She seemed pretty intent on holding her stomach in her hands, trying not to complain about the rough ride.

Suddenly MaryAnn let out a little yelp, startling Joe.

"Are you okay?" he asked her.

"Yeah, I think so, just felt a weird cramp. Hope it's not gas." She looked over at him and smiled a bit and redirected his attention. "Do you know where we are going?"

"I thought I did, but now I'm not so sure. These dang roads twist all over the place. I thought if we went south, we'd catch the highway again. I hoped the snow would ease up, but the snow is worse, and I have no way to tell which direction we are going. There hasn't been another cross street to take, so all I can do is go back or continue."

"Let's continue," MaryAnn suggested. "The road has to end someplace or go someplace."

Joe had to slow down dramatically as visibility was becoming impossible and his car was slipping on the occasional rises in the road. He looked at his cell phone, but there was no service this far away from the city, especially in the low areas. He was considering looking for a farmhouse to ask for directions. As he was wondering what else he could do to get MaryAnn to the city, she yelped again, then grabbed her stomach and groaned.

Joe looked at MaryAnn's wincing face and holding her belly. He was starting to get the full picture of what was going on, so he asked her point-blank, "Are you pregnant?"

MaryAnn made a troubled face and told him, "I never wanted to say anything because I didn't believe it. They said I was the day you found me puking on the tree. I thought it was a mix-up at the clinic. Honestly, Joe, I have nothing to hide. I've never been with a guy. None. Ever."

"Okay, okay. Don't worry about it. It doesn't matter how it happened anyway. If you are having pains and as round as your belly is, you might be in the early stages of labor."

MaryAnn burst into tears. "I don't want to do this, Joe! I don't want to have a kid. I'd rather just be fat. I don't want to do this, not now, not in the snow, not in the middle of nowhere. I should have stayed with Aunt Rachel. She'd know what to do. She wanted me to stay, but I didn't want her to feel mom's wrath. Mom would say it happened on Aunt Rachel's watch, and mom would hate her for it."

Joe tried to calm her as best he could. "I don't think there's much we can do about it now. But I think we really need to find help so we can get to the city. I don't know how far along you are or how your labor is. When did the pain start?"

"It started a few hours ago. I just thought it was gas or cramps or something. Aunt Rachel was going to take me to her doctor after the holiday to make sure what I had. I felt this sort of rumble in my guts once in a while, I kept thinking it was gas, but now it is really uncomfortable." MaryAnn started to groan again holding her belly.

"Oh my God, I need to pray for advice or help or something." Joe was getting into a panic stage but knew he had to keep it together for MaryAnn. He rolled down his window to get some fresh air, hoping it would clear his head for figuring out what to do before MaryAnn had a baby in his car. "There's a rise up ahead in the road. That's about all I can see with my headlight. I'm going to stop up there and see if I can see city lights or get cell reception. I've got to get you to a hospital."

That made MaryAnn burst into more tears. She knew that even though her eighteenth birthday was less than a week away, going to a hospital would involve them notifying her mother, and her father if they could find him. She knew they would hate the child, hate her, hate Joe, and who knows what else.

Joe drove up to the top of the rise in the road and dared to turn off his engine and cut the lights, or light. He got out of the car in the dark silence of being nowhere and looked as hard as he could through the snow and darkness to see if he could see a vehicle headlight or maybe see distant city lights reflecting off the low-hanging clouds....but he saw nothing. He listened for the sounds of traffic but heard nothing. The only thing he could hear was the tittering of snow on the trees and weeds.

He held his cell phone as high in the air as he could reach, somehow thinking it might grab reception, but no bars were showing up, and only a nagging crawl about no connection walked across the screen. He spent a few moments in prayer, asking for at least a crossroad or some kind of sign to tell them where they were or where they were headed. It was cold outside, so he prayed fast and said a quick Amen.

He got back in the car to tell MaryAnn that there was no indication of where they were and that they'd have to keep driving and hopefully hit a small village. "There has to be one. Or a farmhouse. A farmhouse should be easy to find. You know, out in the middle of nowhere farmhouses always have a dusk to dawn light someplace." Joe saw MaryAnn was tensed up with her eyes shut. "Another pain?" MaryAnn nodded. "We need to start keeping track of how far apart they are. Do we count from the start of one to the start of the next one? Or do we count in between?" MaryAnn shrugged her shoulders while exhaling a huge breath.

"I don't know, Joe," MaryAnn said. "I've never done this before. And I don't really want to do this now. I wish there was a hospital around here somewhere."

Joe was trying to remain upbeat and solid, but he was worried like crazy on the inside. He had no clue how to birth a baby. He even shut his eyes when the hamster in his fifth-grade class had babies. Now he was out here with an underage pregnant girl. How the heck was he supposed to deliver a baby, not to mention having to look at those parts of a teenage girl? I'll be arrested and sentenced to life in prison, he thought. He had to find a town or someone to ask for directions. He wished now the sheriff had arrested him. He'd rather be in jail for a headlight out than for human trafficking or kidnapping.

Joe drove on, both of them counting between contractions, and the minutes were becoming shorter. Joe's foot kept trying to increase their speed, so he had to calm himself to drive carefully. The last thing he needed now was to slip off the road. "I can only do about thirty-five before I start slipping," he told her. "I would think a town would be coming up soon." Joe tried to be positive to take MaryAnn's mind off her contractions. Then he saw another rise up ahead where the snow didn't seem as heavy. "I'm going to stop again on that next rise and see if I can see anything or get a cell connection." MaryAnn nodded, groaned again, and looked at the clock.

"Six minutes," she said.

*   *   *

Chapter 20

Light in the Darkness

Dashing through the Snow

*J*oe was doing some serious praying, hoping to see something helpful at the top of the next rise. When he stopped at the top of the little hill, he turned his light out and got out of the car. He left it running this time, worrying that his car might not start again. It was bad enough that his gas level was becoming a concern with just a little better than a quarter of a tank. He shut the car door and breathed in a huge breath of cold, snowy air, and blew it out. He knew he was stressing over this travel arrangement, but he also knew MaryAnn needed help and needed it now. He checked his cell phone. There was no connection at all.

He said a brief prayer again, asking for help, then looked into the distant darkness looking for any sign of city life or even a farmhouse. As his eyes adjusted to the dark, he thought he saw a distant glimmer of light through some trees across a field. Was that a star on the horizon? No, it couldn't be, not with all the snow clouds. Unless it was clearing up in the distance, but he didn't think so. It was heavily overcast with light snow and even some fog, but that glimmer was faintly there and sure looked like a star. In the back of his mind, Joe was aware that it was Christmas Eve and considered his mind might be playing tricks on him. He started to wonder if that glimmering distant light was some kind of mystical beacon from the heavens to flag him down or maybe it was just his imagination, and that glimmer could be a trap drawing them farther from the highway. Joe rethought the craziness of everything he was thinking and that it was just caused by stress and shook it off.

He finally concluded that the light had to be a distant streetlight of some kind. Nothing else made any sense. If it was a streetlight, then it had to be a paved street and most likely would take them to a town. But the light was across the fields, not ahead. There had to be a connecting crossroad. Surely they didn't miss seeing one. Joe decided to continue on hoping for that crossroad soon.

As he got back in the car, he told MaryAnn about the light off in the distance and that he was pretty sure it was a streetlight. He just casually mentioned he thought it might have been a star at first, but it couldn't be with all the clouds and blustery snow. He explained to her the need to find a crossroad that went in the direction of that streetlight. He chunked the shift into drive and started to pick up speed going down the other side of the rise. He silently prayed for a crossroad to show up soon and drove a little faster. MaryAnn was groaning again and crying a bit between groans. He had to get her some medical help.

MaryAnn suddenly shouted, "There!" scaring the daylights out of Joe. She was pointing out the windshield. Sure enough, a green street sign caught his lone headlight. As he drove up to it, it said East-West Post Road.

"That's it!" Joe exclaimed, "We're going that way, to the East! That's generally the direction where I saw the light." And Joe made the turn.

The road to the East was a bit better than the one they had been traveling, so Joe could drive a tad faster. MaryAnn finally saw the light flickering through the trees and agreed it looked like a faint twinkling star. They both felt a sense of relief that there might be help ahead, yet MaryAnn was still worried and plenty scared about what was going to happen very soon. Joe drove carefully, slipping a little on the snowy patches while heading closer to the light. Joe thought to himself about the coincidence of the streetlight resembling the appearance of a star in the East and wondered if it was more than a mere coincidence. He had prayed for help, and now he got a sign, even if it was a street sign, to help him find his way.

They both watched for the light, intermittently seeing it between trees and rolling hills. It became very apparent that it wasn't a star. It looked like any typical streetlight, but they only saw one. Why would there be only one? Joe thought about it. It had to be a light in a barn lot. Joe knew a number of farmers in his church, and they all had a dusk to dawn streetlight in their barn lots or attached to their barns. Still, it was good news. If it was a barn lot light, they would stop and hope the farmer was home to ask directions to the nearest hospital, or maybe they could call the EMTs to come out, or the farmer could shoot them both for trespassing. Joe prayed quietly for a less hostile farmer.

MaryAnn suddenly pointed to a road off to the left that aimed toward the light. "Maybe that is a driveway that will take us to the light on the farm."

There was no street sign for the left turn, and it was a plain gravel road, but they took it on faith that it went to the light. Joe figured if they even got close to a farm, he'd get out of the car and run across a field to the farmhouse....assuming the light was really in a farmer's barn lot. He feared it could be a light left at a deserted oil station or on vacant property.

The few minutes they drove up the road seemed to take forever, especially with MaryAnn's intermittent groaning that now seemed only minutes apart. Even though it was cold, Joe was sweating. He was feeling responsible now and had to do his job. He was a helper of his congregants to get through their troubles, and he was determined to help MaryAnn through hers. Besides, now it was his problem too. He silently prayed as he rumbled over the road, asking God to help him find help.

The road finally took a wide turn and it relieved Joe greatly that the turn was toward the light. As they neared the streetlight, they passed two huge barns, a couple of outbuildings, and lots of white fencing. And thanking God again, he saw that the light was, indeed, a light in a barn lot next to a large, lighted farmhouse.

"Hang on, MaryAnn, help is on the way," he triumphantly said as he approached what looked more like a small parking lot than a driveway with a half dozen vehicles parked. It was lit by the most welcome light he thought any human had ever seen since the shepherds saw the Star in the East. He was excited about getting help quickly and realized he was coming into the drive a little hot, so he barely noticed that the light seemed to be shimmering. Joe didn't have time to consider the oddity, he had a mission to complete, and he was on it, nearly careening into the driveway then slamming the car into park.

"Stay put," he told MaryAnn. "Let me find out if the folks here are friendly and willing to help us!"

*   *   *

Chapter 21

The Farmer and His Wife

The Christmas Party

*J*oe jumped out of the car and ran to the farmhouse porch that was lit pleasantly with old-fashioned Christmas lights and cedar boughs over the doors and windows that he thought looked welcoming. He ran up the steps and tried to knock politely at the door, intent on trying not to scare the daylights out of the folks inside, even though he felt like he wanted to pound the hell out of it. He realized it was near midnight, and most sensible folks were in bed.

While waiting a few seconds between knocking, he could hear a number of adults talking and laughing and soft Christmas carols playing quietly in the background. Then the door suddenly swung open wide. Not a timid crack and peek like many folks would answering a door late at night, but a wide-open welcome. An older woman with her gray hair tied up in a bun raised her eyebrows at the sight of the young man. "Yes?" she asked, "Merry Christmas, young man. What can we do for you?" The talking stopped inside, and only quiet strains of "O Come All Ye Faithful" could be heard in the background. All eyes were on Joe. He could see a half dozen older folks, some with plates of food on their laps, tea cups, or a beer bottle or two, but no children. He reasoned they'd be in bed dreaming of Santa Claus. There was a cozy fire in a large farm fireplace and a real Christmas tree in the corner decorated with old-fashioned electric bulbs. All the ornaments were angels, including the tree topper. The entry and living room were decorated with angels, too, and a large festive buffet table was covered with dishes and trays loaded with treats and foods. Joe said a short prayer to himself then took a deep breath and explained that he is lost and needs to get to the nearest town as quickly as possible.

An older man struggled out of a chair and came to the door by the older lady. "What is the problem? Is there something we can do to help?"

Joe knocked some snow off his hair, and just a hint of his clerical collar could be seen beneath his coat. Both the older lady and older man noticed the collar as Joe responded to their questions.

"I have a young lady in the car that really needs a doctor or a hospital as soon as possible. We were headed to the city medical center, but I got off the highway at the wrong place and never could figure out how to get back. I have no navigation aids, and my cell phone hasn't been getting reception. If you could just tell me how to get back on the highway or to the next town, I'd be grateful." Joe heard MaryAnn groan in the car and hoped the old people didn't hear it.

"Your lady friend sounds awfully sick," the older lady said. "I'm going to go have a look." She grabbed a shawl and threw it over her shoulders and jammed her feet into boots that were standing next to the door.

Joe wanted to stop her, but he knew he was out of luck and out of time. He knew he was in over his head and needed help. His prayer was for help, and maybe this is what was sent to him.

"Well, son," the old man started to explain, "you are a long way to the highway, maybe forty minutes in this weather, and probably another thirty to the city."

The older lady opened MaryAnn's car door and talked to MaryAnn for barely a minute when she shouted to the old man, "This young lady is in labor. She'll never make it to the city in this weather, and EMTs will never get here either."

The older man, noticing the rattrap of Joe's car, told him it would be a dangerous drive with the gathering snow and the hills they would have to deal with on the way. If he got stuck or slid off the road, it could be hours before help arrived because cell communication out this far is iffy. And that is on a good day.

Joe cringed as now the secret was out. He couldn't leave MaryAnn, but maybe he should. They will probably want to call MaryAnn's mother or call an ambulance. Then it would all wind up with legal problems from MaryAnn not being eighteen. His life with the church would be over, and who knows what else.

"Let's get the young lady out of the car," the older lady said as she started to help MaryAnn with the seat belt.

MaryAnn grabbed the lady's wrist to stop her. "No. Joe is going to take me to a doctor in the city," she informed the older lady.

"How far apart are your contractions?" the older lady asked.

"About five minutes or so. We should have another hour to make it to the city."

The older lady made a troubled face. "You don't have an hour."

*　　*　　*

Chapter 22

No Room in the Inn

Is it an Outhouse?

MaryAnn's face gave the older lady all the information she needed to know about how scared the girl was, and she obviously needed help. The older lady started at the beginning by asking MaryAnn, "Do your parents know about this?"

"No."

"Okay. Well, we can call them and..."

"NO!" MaryAnn yelled, then spoke softer, "no, no, please don't call my mother. I'll be 18 in a few days, and I'll be legal then to make my own life."

"But honey, you are going to have a baby. How do you think you and this young man are going to manage on the run?"

"We aren't on the run. I am. That's Joe. I asked him to help me get to the city. He's the kindest person I know."

"Is he the father?"

MaryAnn thought about the consequences of her answer to that and decided to dodge it. "No, it was someone else."

"Should that someone else be notified?"

"No." MaryAnn started to groan loudly.

"Okay then, young lady..." the older lady patted MaryAnn's hands, "...okay, we'll do what we can. My name is Sarah. We need to get you out of the car."

A much older, wrinkled lady hobbled to the doorway from her rocker, leaning hard on a wooden cane. "What is going on?" her voice crackled as she smacked the cane on the open door jamb, "You keeping the door open to heat the fields?"

The man in the house hollered back, "Aw ma, go sit. We're going to have some company." The older man introduced himself to Joe, "I'm Harry. Sarah here is my wife. That's my mom, Agnes, yelling at us. Over there, that's my twin sister, Harriet, and her husband, John. The guy with the pie, that's Jake. He's a widower from down the road, and Annie, the lady with the apron, she's my wife's sister. We get together every Christmas for as long as I can remember.

Joe admired their strength of character and joy of life as he introduced himself around.

"If ya hungry, Mom has some stew over there in the crockpot," John pointed as he headed toward a tray of cookies.

"I'm good," Joe said. "I'm too worried and nervous to think about food right now."

Sarah and Harriet were helping MaryAnn up the porch steps and into the house. "Hey everyone, this is ..... well, young lady, I don't believe we have your name yet."

"I'm MaryAnn, your party killer."

"Oh, I don't think so, MaryAnn. You came to the right place," Sarah said.

"I think she is going to get a Christmas gift very soon!" Harry announced.

Sarah made him shush up. "This is not the time, Harry."

They brought out a kitchen chair for MaryAnn to sit on then Sarah and Harry went to the kitchen to talk quietly about what they could do for this young girl. MaryAnn felt another contraction coming, and she panicked at all the strangers looking at her. She started to cry and groan at the same time. Sarah came rushing out of the kitchen with a plan.

"Here's what we're going to do. This is a farm. We've worked this farm for generations and have birthed nearly every critter that ever came here. We've never lost a lamb, never lost a goat, never lost a horse or a cow or a cat. I think we can do this here.

MaryAnn became alarmed... "Here?" looking around at the living room.

"Oh no," Sarah explained. "We have a guest cottage in the back. We've been using it for storage and just let our guests stay in the big house seeing how we're all family. Because of our holiday company, we don't have any more places in the house, but there's plenty of room in the guest cottage where you'll have some privacy, but we'll have to do some quick rearranging."

John and Harry were already putting on coats and hats as they headed out to make room in the guest house. Sarah excused herself, "I need to get some clean blankets and bedding. There's no electric out there, but there is a small pot belly stove for heat."

"I'll go with the guys and help move things," Joe said as

he followed them through the kitchen and out the back door.

"I feel terrible being such a pain. This is Christmas Eve. I can stay in Joe's car," MaryAnn said.

"Nonsense. Because this is Christmas Eve, it makes it that much more important to share everything we can," Sarah said. "This is a time for prayers to be answered."

MaryAnn suddenly grabbed her belly and doubled over groaning. Harriet grabbed her coat saying she'd make sure the guys are getting things done.

As Sarah came down from upstairs with her arms loaded with linens and blankets, she offered MaryAnn something to eat. Even though the food on the dining room table and the buffet looked spectacular, MaryAnn couldn't even think about eating right now.

Grandma Agnes was staring at the young girl for a long few minutes, then hollered loudly to Sarah, "You gonna need to get that girl to the outhouse before she drops a calf right here." Then she sipped her tea, looking over the top of the cup at MaryAnn.

"Outhouse?" MaryAnn repeated, looking at Sarah.

"Don't worry. It's not an outhouse," Sarah consoled. "Harry's mother's mind isn't what it used to be. We haven't had an outhouse for decades. This is a small guest cottage. We used to have farmhands come help at busy times of the year, so we built a little place for them to be reasonably comfortable. The barn shop has accommodations, too, but it can only fit two, so we added the cottage. Harry's mother always referred to it as the "out" house because, to her, it is out of this house. Come now, we should be heading out there so you can get comfortable...well, as comfortable as we can make it.

MaryAnn struggled to get out of the chair but was

determined and was concerned that Joe had left her with these strangers. Even though they seemed very nice, she had seen movies where nice situations can be deceiving and turn into a nightmare.

*   *   *

Chapter 23

Accommodating Accommodations

Come Unto Him all ye who Labor

Sarah helped MaryAnn through the kitchen, out the back door, and down the little sidewalk path to the backyard, where MaryAnn could see the barn lot light up high on its pole, shining down, lighting their way along the little walkway of shoveled snow. MaryAnn could see the guesthouse, and yes, it was more like a tiny cottage, even having little shutters on the window and a little porch across the front.

It wasn't quite warm on the inside, but a young man was building a fire in the potbelly stove. All MaryAnn could tell about the young man from the back was that he had the blondest hair she'd ever seen. It almost looked golden when backlit by the fire he was lighting in the stove.

Harriet was taking the large dust covers off the few pieces of furniture and folding them carefully. Harry and Joe were carrying some boxes and stacking them up in the rear while Annie lit the kerosene lamps. It wasn't a very big place, but big enough to be reasonably comfortable and private. Sarah made MaryAnn sit while she and her sister-in-law put clean bedding on the bed, fluffed the pillows, and added a couple of quilts. By now, the men were standing around looking helpless when Sarah told them all to go back to the house and get something to eat. "You too, Gabe. Thanks for getting the stove going."

As the men were leaving, Joe gave MaryAnn a hug and whispered to her, "I believe these are good folks. God gave us this break so trust them." And Joe left with the other men.

After the men left, the young farmhand lagged behind and asked Sarah, "Is she going to be okay?"

"I'm pretty sure she's going to be just fine, Gabe."

"Thank you, Sarah," he said. "Thank you for taking good care of the girl."

"Go up to the house," Sarah told him, "and get something to eat with the guys."

Gabe had stoked a good hot fire in the potbelly stove. MaryAnn could feel the warmth radiating from it when another contraction hit, and she doubled up moaning.

"Come, young lady," Sarah said. "It's time to get yourself ready to receive your gift." As they helped MaryAnn into the bed, another contraction interfered with her wanting to curl up and go to sleep and pretend this all wasn't happening, but more kept coming.

Sarah and Harriet cranked up the wicks on both kerosene lanterns. With no electricity in the guest house, the kerosene lanterns would have to do. Harriet brought one over to MaryAnn's bed. She saw that MaryAnn was freaking out at facing what was coming with total strangers around and started to cry.

"It's all right," Sarah said, trying to comfort MaryAnn. "If you were at a hospital there'd be at least a half dozen strangers looking at you. There's only me, Harriet, and Annie, and we'll be your guides. Harriet brought a warm quilt to cover MaryAnn for some privacy when MaryAnn let loose with a giant grunting moan.

Annie commented on the contractions being very close together, so Harriet tried to take MaryAnn's mind off the discomfort and told her, "You know, back in the days of the early prairie, women usually had their children with a midwife, a grandma, or the oldest daughter helping out. It was natural. Today, young ladies go to the hospital, and it's all done in a medical situation. This will be so much better. It will be quieter, peaceful, and more relaxing than a hospital."

"This doesn't seem peaceful nor relaxing!" MaryAnn grunted out as a contraction subsided. "I'd really rather be at a hospital. They would knock me out."

Sarah had some necessary tools and a pail of hot water she'd put on the potbelly stove to sterilize everything when MaryAnn interrupted with another contraction.

"That was only two minutes," Harriet said. "Let's get her ready."

MaryAnn began to grunt louder at the next contraction. The older ladies were excited to be part of this process, but MaryAnn just wanted to get it over with. She just about got her breath from one contraction when another started winding up.

Back at the house, they could faintly hear MaryAnn. Joe felt miserable to hear her, but Harry said, "This is what women do. When Sarah had her baby, we had a midwife, and Sarah was tough, but still, at the end, she was hollerin' at us all, even did some cussin'."

"How many children do you have?" Joe asked, noticing that no one in the living room was young enough to be one of his children.

"Well, Joe, we don't have any." Harry took a pipe off the fireplace mantle, tamped it down, lit it, and took a few puffs. "Sarah only had the one child. The child died when she was about two. The influenza. We couldn't get a doctor out here back then. Sarah was young, almost a kid herself. But she never got pregnant again. Not like we weren't tryin'. She said God was punishing her for letting her baby get sick." Harry got lost in his memories and slumped in a dining room chair, puffing his pipe and pondering his life. Gramma Agnes didn't let it go.

"Yep, if Sarah would have fed that baby better and kept her warm enough, she wouldn't a-died. That poor thing suffered a long time." Gramma Agnes wiped her nose with an embroidered hankie.

Harry commented, "Ma's memory may be bad, but she apparently remembers that event quite well." He took a few more pipe puffs giving his mother a dry look. "It was a sad time, but we went on with the farmin'. I always hoped we'd get another kid. I would have liked to have a son or two. I wouldn't have to hire helpers...." he stopped when he heard MaryAnn hollering, almost screaming.

"...any time now...." Harry's voice faded off.

Joe sat with his hands folded, saying secret prayers in his head and praying that he did the right thing.

*   *   *

Chapter 24

Count Your Blessings

Instead of Sheep

The women were watching over Mary-Ann, counting contractions with her and dabbing her sweaty forehead, when they heard a light tap on the cottage door. Annie cracked the door a bit. It was Gabe standing there holding something bundled in burlap.

"She was born a bit too soon, and it's too cold for her in the barn..." Gabe explained to Annie. "We usually use the cottage on cold nights to warm up the early lambs." His bundle let out a tiny bleat. Annie motioned Gabe inside and shut the door to the cold.

"Can I see her?" MaryAnn asks between panting breaths.

Gabe pulled back a corner of the burlap revealing a tiny newborn lamb's face. Her snowy white face, pink nose, and curious black eyes looked so adorable that MaryAnn asked the women to make a place for the lamb. The women agreed, and Gabe rummaged in a box bringing up two old blankets. He made a place in the corner by the pot belly stove for the lamb. She let out a tiny bleat as if to say thank you. MaryAnn looked at the tiny bundle in the corner with a worried look. The young man could see

MaryAnn's concern, and he tried to comfort her, saying, "Don't worry, if we can keep her warm tonight, she'll be okay."

After he settled the lamb, Gabe removed his hat and twisted it nervously in his hands, looking at MaryAnn. Sarah made introductions. "MaryAnn, this is Gabe, our farm hand. Gabe, this is MaryAnn. She was a stranger that stopped by, and we are helping her tonight." Even though MaryAnn was seriously preoccupied with her task at hand, she could see Gabe was a very fair-skinned but attractive young man with that beautiful blonde hair that almost appeared to be glowing in the firelight of the cottage

"Nice to meet you," Gabe said to MaryAnn in an unusually musical voice. "Sorry to interrupt the occasion."

"It's fine," Sarah said. "Did you get up to the house to get something to eat yet? There's enough food for an army on the buffet in the dining room."

"Thank you, Ma'am. I had some earlier. It was terrific home-cooked food."

All smiles were interrupted by MaryAnn letting out a loud groan. Sarah shooed Gabe out, and the women got ready for their work.

*   *   *

Chapter 25

What Child is This?

... so tender and mild

It wasn't long before MaryAnn was in the process of delivering a precious little infant. MaryAnn could see the light in the barn lot through the frost on the window pane. She believed it looked just like the star in the East that shone over Bethlehem on the night of an extraordinary child's birth. She thought briefly that the light's radiance was a miracle of everything that had fallen into place on this cold Christmas Eve night. It only took a few more minutes and a push for the baby to emerge into the lantern light of the cottage. The three ladies sighed and were relieved it all went well. They wrapped the baby in a towel and tucked the little bundle into MaryAnn's arms. MaryAnn was instantly and totally enchanted by the little one counting fingers and toes.

Ten! The fingers counted up to ten, and MaryAnn was glad this was over. She glanced back to the light in the barn lot as though it was some kind of blessing shining down on them all, and she thought she could almost see the formation of the Christmas star in the light. As she gazed at it radiating over the farm, she saw a dark, hunched shadow approaching outside and felt a sting of fear. The cottage door handle slowly turned, and the door opened so slowly, but all three women noticed it. Harriet finally grabbed the knob and yanked it open....and

Grandma Agnes clumsily stumbled in with her cane coming in first. Harriet caught her from falling to the floor.

"I was leanin' on that dang knob, Harriet!" she shouted. MaryAnn couldn't help but chuckle. The old grandma just wanted to see the baby. Grandma Agnes shook it off while holding an armload of linens, "I brung a couple clean dish towels to make a diaper," her raspy voice spoke as she handed them to Sarah.

"This is nice," Sarah said and started a little linen origami, trying to fold one of the towels in numerous ways to try to fit the tiny infant.

Grandma Agnes watched for a while but got fed up with Sarah fiddling with the towel forever and yanked it out of her hand. "You young folk don't know jack these days," and she quickly folded it to fit the baby perfectly, then used two of her hairpins to secure the diaper. She expertly swaddled the infant in a few more clean towels. Grandma kissed the baby's head, as did Sarah, Annie, and Harriet, and they handed the cleaned-up tiny bundle to MaryAnn. The baby made a little cry, and MaryAnn was overcome with emotion.

Annie returned to the house and quickly came back to the cottage with one of Grandma Agnes' flannel nightgowns, fresh sheets, and a warm quilt.

"Congratulations, young lady. You did a tough job tonight," Annie said and could not resist stroking the baby's cheek gently and cooing to the infant softly. "You call me Auntie Annie; if that's okay with your mother."

Mother? MaryAnn cringed thinking she was now a "mother," but she had to shake off the bad memories and come to terms with it all. "I'll be happy for the baby to call you all aunties and uncles. You are all such wonderful people to do so much on a holiday when you have company. I'll never be able to thank you enough."

"Shhhh," Sarah said as she busied managing everything quietly. "No thanks are needed. We were in the right place at the right time for you and the little one. This is a gift to all of us."

MaryAnn relaxed a bit and snuggled her newborn, realizing she was in the care of some very benevolent people. The women assisted in cleaning up and getting MaryAnn back into bed, clean and tired. As the women tucked MaryAnn in, she noticed the quilt had the same fresh outdoor smell of Aunt Rachel's bedding and the quilt pattern was of angels and pine trees. It seemed these farm folks had angels everywhere. Maybe that's what gave this place a sense of wonder where she felt truly blessed this night. Even so, she was aware of the near future. She knew she could not wear out her welcome with the farmer and his family and wondered how she was going to manage having nothing for the baby and nowhere to go. She knew Joe would have to get back to the town and his church duties.

Auntie Annie was grinning from ear to ear gazing at the baby. MaryAnn suggested she hold the infant for a bit and Auntie Annie was thrilled to take the bundle and began to sway a little side to side, humming a tune while MaryAnn looked out the window at the light in the barn lot, wondering how she could get a job with a new baby to manage.

Sarah finally had things organized to suit her when she sat on the edge of the bed. "I have to apologize that since we don't have any children or grandchildren, we have nothing handy for the baby. The city is a half-day drive to get supplies, and tomorrow is Christmas Day, so everything will be closed, but we'll all put our heads together and figure out something."

*   *   *

Chapter 26

Meanwhile, Back at the House

Tree for Two

*M*eanwhile back at the house, everyone noticed the sounds had stopped from the cottage. Gabe patted Joe on the back, "Congratulations, man. You're a father!"

"Uh, no," Joe told him, "I'm not a Father yet. I'm just the assistant pastor, and we don't call the reverend a Father as......" Joe cut himself off when he realized what Gabe meant. "Oh, sorry. No, I'm not the father of MaryAnn's child. Like I said, I'm the assistant pastor of our town chapel. This young lady needed help and called me. So I was giving her a ride to the city hospital."

Gabe raised an eyebrow and smiled. "Ok. Your story. But you'll see one day."

Farmer Harry put his pipe down and spoke to the air, "I think this infant needs a Christmas tree. It is the child's first Christmas. There should be a tree. Gabe, give me a hand," he said as he started to put on his coat, scarf, galoshes, and a hat with earflaps.

"Yes, sir!" Gabe said as he jumped to bundle up again.

Grandma Agnes had shuffled back to the kitchen as the men were heading back out. "What are you two up to now?"

"The child should have a tree!" Gabe said as they left.

"Yes indeed," Grandma Agnes said. She thought for a moment and started rummaging in the kitchen cupboards for something.

It wasn't long when Farmer Harry and Gabe knocked on the cottage door with a freshly cut little cedar tree. Grandma Agnes was shuffling close behind.

"Oh my," Sarah said as she opened the door, and the men shuffled in with the little tree. "What a lovely idea. But this young lady needs some rest."

"Sarah," Gabe said, "it'll only take a minute or two, and Harry said this child needs a tree on the first Christmas. I have a spare string of twinkle lights in the back that we can drape on the tree."

Grandma Agnes followed the tree in and had her apron clutched to her chest with something in it. Sarah looked at her with amused suspicion as Grandma Agnes sheepishly lowered her apron. They all saw she brought Christmas-shaped cookie cutters from the kitchen. "We don't have much else," she said, "and the little tree should have some ornaments." Sarah smiled and told her to go ahead and decorate the tree. Gabe came back with a small strand of old twinkle lights tangled in a knot.

"I hope they work. They've been in the back since....." Gabe stopped himself and looked at Sarah.

"It's okay, Gabe. That was a long time ago. The lights are fine."

Gabe did a patient de-tangling of the lights, then put them on the little tree and ran an extension cord from the light pole outside and under the door to plug them in. The lights worked, and everyone oohed and ahhed. Grandma

Agnes started humming "O Tannenbaum" as she carefully arranged the cookie cutters. As she placed the last one, she stood back, "There. Very nice."

The women thanked Grandma Agnes for her idea, and MaryAnn was feeling overwhelmed with the good spirit of these strangers.

"Thank you all," MaryAnn whispered in grateful joy. She cried softly remembering so many horrible Christmases with her uncaring, selfish mother. But tonight felt like the best Christmas in the world, here, with strangers, her newborn, and the tiny tree.

* * *

Chapter 27

Incoming!

Keep On Truckin'

*B*ack at the farmhouse, things had quieted down. There was some yawning and a little nodding off now and then. It looked like everyone was thinking about going to bed when Jake commented on hearing distant rumbling. One by one, they stopped to listen to what was happening.

"What is that, an earthquake?" Joe asked as the coffee in his cup began shivering.

"I don't know," John said. "I never heard it before. It sounds like it's getting louder. Whatever it is, it's coming closer."

They knew the highway was a long way out, so it couldn't be highway traffic, but they were intent on finding out what the rumbling was, so they all spilled out onto the front porch to see what was coming.

"Sounds like an airplane coming in for a landing to me," Harry said as he kept looking into the darkness. It wasn't long before Harry let out a long whistle of wonder. "Well, I'll be jiggered! Looks like someone else lost their way tonight."

I'll be jiggered? Joe thought. Who says that these days? But Joe got sidetracked by the oncoming rush of noise and rumbling.

They all watched as down the road and out of the darkness, headlights glimmered through the trees and brush with the sound of big tires grinding on the gravel. The racket rocked the night as the machines approached the farm, breaking the silence of the snowfall with heavy motors thundering forward. One by one, three loaded tractor-trailers with all their cab and trailer lights lit up like a traveling carnival rolled into view. At first, slowing their trucks on the gravel, then spewing their air brakes and finally grinding to a halt out on the road in front of the farmhouse. Then everything was relatively quiet except for the diesels still idling. When, in a very short minute, the doors of the cabs flew open, and the hearty drivers jumped out, shouting Merry Christmas and waving to the men on the porch.

The drivers made their way to the porch introducing themselves along the way, Mark, Luke, and Matt, and they were welcomed by everyone from the house with lots of handshaking and cheerful holiday greetings among them. Farmer Harry welcomed them into the farmhouse, and introductions were made all around while the truckers were explaining that Luke, their lead truck driver, was tired and got off the highway at the wrong place.

"We drive for King Transport. We came in from New Jersey and have been driving for two days. We were trying to make this last leg on our schedule and were pushing to get it done," Mark said. "I guess we got too tired. Once we discovered the error, we couldn't find a place to turn our rigs around. We needed to find a big enough parking lot to make the turns. With everything covered in snow, we didn't want to try to make a turn where we couldn't see the surface under the snow. So we saw your light way off through the trees, and at first, we weren't even sure it was a light or a star, but we followed the light hoping it would be at a place that might have the space for us to turn our rigs to get back on the interstate."

Harry pointed to the dining room table and offered them some hot beef stew from the big crockpot and warm homemade bread. Matt's eyes lit up brighter than the Christmas tree while Mark said, "This is terrific to have some home-cooked food for a change." He continued chatting with Farmer Harry, explaining how they saw his barn lot light and how the old-fashioned Christmas lights on the house made it look so warm and friendly.

Luke took a huge bite of bread then tried to talk with his mouth full, to remind Mark about moving the trucks. "Dom't forget to ask aboud da bess way back to da innerstate and if we can durn our rigs in da bahn lot." Matt and Mark started laughing at Luke's cheeks puffed out with the warm bread, sounding like he ate a pillow.

While the three truckers loaded up their plates with steaming hot stew, Grandma Agnes sliced three more big slabs of the warm homemade bread for them, and Harry told the truckers they were welcome to use the barn lot to turn their rigs around after a little car shuffling.

"Appreciate it, Harry," Matt said, "and appreciate the home-cooked meal. This is quite a treat and a real gift for us road warriors. And I must say, this is the best Christmas Eve any of us that drive over the holidays has ever had. It's a miracle that anyone was even up at this hour, let alone have a spread of food out like this." Mark and Luke tapped their spoons on their plates in applause and agreement.

"This is really good stew, and the bread is fantastic!" Luke commented now that he'd swallowed the bread.

"And how!" Joe added as he wiped up the last of his stew gravy with a chunk of bread. "Not much of anything is better than home cooking. I'll be thanking the ladies for sure."

"I'm sure they'll appreciate the thanks," Harry said. "We didn't go to bed because we still had a job or two left to do." Harry told the truckers about Joe and how he had come an hour earlier with a young lady in labor. "With the weather and the distance to the city, we thought it was best to have her remain here rather than gamble on the roads." Harry went on to tell them about the young couple, and now the young lady and her baby are out in the guest cottage.

Joe listened to Harry telling the truckers the story of MaryAnn's newborn, and he became aware of the odd coincidence of the King truckers coming from the East, the East coast anyway. And three of them. It was too ridiculous to bother saying anything.

The truckers were having a good conversation about trucking over pie and coffee with John and Jake. They explained they carried supplies for independent discount stores across the nation and were on the road most of the year. They always seemed to get stuck with driving over the holidays.

Gabe came in the back door from the cottage and took off his hat and coat as Annie was arranging more pie slices on plates. Joe and the three truckers looked almost bewildered at Gabe and his nearly golden hair and practically glowing pale face. Gabe noticed he was being stared at, so he diverted the attention by singing a silly version of "I Saw Three Ships" but rewording it. "I heard three trucks on Christmas Day, on Christmas Day, on Christmas Day, I heard three trucks on Christmas Day, on Christmas Day in the morning." he smiled and chuckled. "It is Christmas morning, isn't it?"

"It will be in a few minutes," Harry said. "Coffee and pie are up."

"Thank you, Harry," Gabe said. "I could use some coffee. I don't get it often."

Joe thanked Gabe for MaryAnn's little tree and kept staring at him. "You have the most amazing hair," Joe commented.

Gabe blew the comment off with a quick thank-you and made a brief comment that it was probably just the lights in the Christmas tree. Joe wasn't so sure but let it alone.

While the truckers were enjoying their hot meal, John, Jake, and Joe got their coats on to go shuffle cars. Joe asked Gabe if he was going to come, but Harry mentioned that Gabe didn't drive. Joe noted it and thought it was odd that someone on a farm didn't drive but went out with the other guys to move the cars.

As the truckers finished eating, they offered to help clean up the dishes until Harry told them to let it be. That was the job of the ladies, and they were particular about how it was done.

*   *   *

Chapter 28

Bearing Gifts

The truckers prepared to be on their way and were shaking hands all around and wishing everyone a Merry Christmas and Happy New Year, even having a few man-hugs and hearty back-pats. As the truckers were leaving, Harry went out on the porch, taking a couple of puffs of his pipe while waiting for them to get to their trucks. He wanted to watch them turn those big rigs around. But the truckers were standing in front of one of the trucks and having a brief discussion. The three separated to their individual trucks, but instead of getting in the cabs, they all went to the trailers.

"What are they doing?" Joe asked Harry as he came out to see why the front door was still open.

"I'm not sure. Probably doing a pre-flight check on their rigs. I'm sure the roads rattled them around like Yahtzee dice in a cup, and they want to make sure all is well before heading back. A little prevention is worth a pound of salami, ya know."

Joe looked at Harry, wondering if he was being funny, tired, or losing his marbles. Joe guessed that Harry and Sarah had to be at least in their late seventies, so anything was possible.

They watched the truckers open the doors of their trailers and climb up. No doubt to check on shifting loads.

It wasn't long before everyone could hear the huge trailer doors slamming shut, echoing through the snow and trees. The truckers rejoined each other and came tromping through the snow heading back to the porch.

"Are you lost already?" Harry hollered across the yard. "You never even got behind the wheel."

"No," Mark yelled back. "We had to figure out a way to thank you for your hospitality to strangers late at night."

"We don't mind," Farmer Harry said as they approached the porch. "We should all give a little now and then to help out our fellow man."

"That's true," Luke said. "And that's just what we're going to do since you wouldn't let us do the dishes. We thought of another way to show our appreciation." All three truckers had some things under their jackets and coats that they apparently took from the trailers of their rigs.

"We'd like to honor the newborn with your permission. We have a few things the infant might be able to use in the coming days," Mark said. "Since we have supplies for discount stores, we have an array of product lines, and we chose a few for the baby and mother."

"Well, that's nice and all, but.... " Harry started to say he didn't think stolen things would be a good way to start out life, but Mark cut him off.

"Don't worry. We aren't stealing anything. The cost will be deducted from the shipment. Everything will be accounted for and deducted from our checks when we dock and unload, and we don't mind. We have so much, and I'm sure that little baby came with nothing."

"You are right about that," Farmer Harry said, "The young lady came with nothing too."

"Well, there you are," Luke said. Can you show us where to go and introduce us?"

* * *

Chapter 29

Santa Clauses Coming to Town

The Finest Gifts We Bring

Farmer Harry grabbed his coat again and led the three truckers through the house and out to the cottage. Joe went along so MaryAnn wouldn't feel confronted by a bunch of big guys she hadn't met yet. They went across the yard to the cottage like a train of Christmas rail cars, with Harry and his smoking pipe as the locomotive and Joe in the rear as the caboose. When they got to the cottage, Harry tapped lightly on the door.

"Shhhh," Sarah said as she quietly opened the door. "Baby and mother are napping. She's had a stressful few days, I imagine."

MaryAnn wasn't napping and heard the door opening, "Thank you, Sarah," MaryAnn whispered, "but I'm not sleeping. I'm just resting my eyes and trying to figure out what I'm going to do next. Let them come in."

"Who are these other men?" Sarah asked Harry.

"They are truckers. We got them some supper, and they want to pay back some thanks."

Sarah let Harry and Joe in, followed by the three truckers with their arms clutching their coats and jackets that appeared stuffed. They all squoze into the small cottage space, keeping a safe distance from the potbelly stove after Luke got a bit too close.

"These guys would like to see the baby," Harry said to MaryAnn. "These guys are truckers that got lost from the highway and followed the light in the barn lot just like you and Joe did."

MaryAnn unwrapped some of the towels so the truckers could see the little one.

Luke knelt down close and took MaryAnn's hand in his. "Hello, my dear. Congratulations on the baby. My name is Luke, Luke Gould. I'm one of three truckers that accidentally drove up here somehow, and we heard of your newborn and your situation. As a little Christmas gift for you and the baby, I have a few things from our baby wares collection and a gift card here that a guy gave me that was thankful I didn't crush his loading dock. Get yourself something, and something for the baby too."

MaryAnn was surprised and touched when she saw all the baby items he was pulling out from under his coat and out of his pockets. "I appreciate your kind thoughts, but I don't want to take your stuff. I'll figure out what I have to do later."

"Listen, my dear," Luke told her, "maybe it's no coincidence we were led here. We've never made a driving error in all the years we've been trucking. Please accept our little gifts so we can feel like we did something good this Christmas. It is a traditional time of gift-giving." Luke leaned over and kissed the baby's head.

MaryAnn nodded okay as a few tears started to form and her nose began to sting, the usual sign of her emotions welling up again.

"Sorry for the tears," MaryAnn said. "I'm not sad. I think it might be all the hormones or something." But everyone knew it was something else, like love, joy, and sincere appreciation.

"I wish I had something to give to you," she said to Luke. "But I don't have anything." MaryAnn thought for a minute and asked if someone would go back to Joe's car and get her the bag she threw in the back seat. Harriet grabbed her coat and volunteered to run the mission while MaryAnn thanked Luke over and over for each item she received.

Mark then took his turn and sat on the edge of MaryAnn's bed as he introduced himself. "I'm Mark Murphy, and you should have the Merriest of Christmases ever," he said as he began pulling more little packages of infant items out from under his coat. Then added, "Ho, ho, ho!" a few times as he pulled more packages of baby items out of his pockets. "Just have a Merry Christmas, young lady, and I hope these things help out."

MaryAnn thanked him as he handed her each package. She was becoming excited about having so many new things for her baby. Booties, a few bottles, little blankets, tiny shirts, she kept picking up the packages and sorting through them all.

Matt tapped Mark on the shoulder and told him to scoot over. "Hi, I'm Matthew Franken," he said as he continued to nudge Mark out of the way. "I drive with these guys, and I gotta admit that it is so strange for us to have gotten off the highway like we did. But look at it now, it's a miracle for all of us." He handed her packages of personal grooming products and a few new T-shirts, and a sweatshirt for herself. "Hope everything fits. And here is a burner phone. Joe told me you don't have a cell phone, so you can use this. I carry these cheapies in the cab in case I leave my cell at a truck stop a hundred miles back. If you have someone you'd like to call or text in an emergency, use it. It's good for about a month and maybe an hour of talk time, then you throw it out.

"This is all just too much," MaryAnn said through happy tears. "It is all so wonderful and so thoughtful. These will be God-given, or trucker-given, gifts to help me as I try to start a new life with my baby."

Harriet got back to the cottage with the bag MaryAnn asked for and handed it to her. MaryAnn sat up and rummaged in the bag and pulled out three packages of Razzies. She handed one to each trucker, hugging them, thanking them, and wishing them Merry Christmas too. The truckers acted all shy and silly, accepting MaryAnn's small token of thanks. Everyone was chuckling over it when they all heard a big crash over their heads up in the small attic of the cottage.

Sarah's concern was imminent as she rushed to the back of the cottage and noticed the pull-down attic steps were down.

*   *   *

Chapter 30

Cradle of Civilization

The Classic Rock

"Is that you up there, Harry?" Sarah shouted. "Are you okay?"

"Yeah," She heard Harry grunt a few more times and some plunking of heavy items in the attic.

"What on earth are you doing up there? It's cold!"

Sarah could hear a lot of clattering and something heavy being dragged across the floor up there. Harry finally appeared at the top of the steps. "I have something for the young lady."

"What on earth could you have shoved up there that the young lady would possibly want?" Sarah asked.

After a little more struggling, shuffling, and dragging, Harry said, "This!" as he dragged something to the top of the steps.

Sarah instantly got tears in her eyes. "You saved it?" she said. "You saved it after all these many, many, years?"

"Yep. Always thought it might come in handy one day.

Today is the day," Harry said as he began to wrangle a wooden cradle down the steps to the floor, then pushed the drop-down steps back up in position.

He hugged Sarah as she whimpered a bit and glanced at the cradle. Harry looked at her for a few moments, and finally, she nodded. "Yes. It is time."

The two each took an end of the cradle and brought it out to MaryAnn.

MaryAnn could not believe what she was seeing, a beautifully carved old-fashioned cradle with exquisitely carved angels on the headboard and meticulously carved scrollwork on the sides. Her heart was so full, and she was so overwhelmed with all the gifts she broke down in real tears. Sarah sat at the edge of the bed with her own tears and comforted MaryAnn with some hugs.

As the packed house stepped back to give the cradle room, Harry cleared his throat and tried to secretly wipe away one of his tears as everyone stood silent when he began to speak.

"I hand-carved this cradle many, MANY years ago when I was a young man with strong and nimble hands, and Sarah was going to give me a son or daughter. It took me months to do it right. I whittled the wood pegs to hold it together and carved all the decorations you see on it. I carefully sanded it smooth and oil-rubbed it until every inch of it glowed. I see it needs a little cleanup now, a scrubbing bath, and oil rubbing to preserve the wood again, and it should be good and as beautiful as the day I finished it. When I presented it to Sarah the night our child was born, it was like a communion of the spirits of the three of us, making us an unbroken circle of family."

Harry continued, "It was a long process to build, but I looked forward to working on it a little every day. I started by choosing an oak tree from our land and, from it, created the base and spindles. I used oak not only for its strength but also because, in Greek mythology, it represented the power of Zeus. Throughout history, oak trees represented honor, nobility, wisdom, and long life, all virtues we wanted for our child. So the oak I chose first. Then I chose a Hazel tree for the decorative planks, Hazel is hardwood, and the cutting went slow with only the hand tools that were available. The Hazel tree is considered the tree of knowledge and inspiration in Irish traditions, and we wanted that for our child too. Then I spent months carefully hand-carving the angels for the headboard. I chose the Hawthorn tree wood for those angels. Hawthorn trees provide protection, luck, and prosperity to those that gather below them. And all the trim and scrolls I carved from a German Linden tree. It is known for truth, justice, wisdom, and benevolent protection. I wanted all these qualities for our child.

It is important for an infant to be surrounded by love from family and friends. I also believe a newborn needs to be surrounded by nature's steadfast presence and have the protection of the Earth we live on as well." Harry looked wistfully at the cradle, "I almost chopped it into kindling wood after our child died, but something told me to save it, something special would come along one day and the cradle would be needed again. Today is that day. I knew it the moment MaryAnn stepped into our home."

Almost everyone was wiping tears away as Sarah and Harriet took the cradle back to the house to clean it up. As talk quieted down, the truckers began telling MaryAnn goodbye and good luck and headed back to the house. MaryAnn couldn't say enough thank-yous.

Joe stood there in the cottage after everyone left, scratching his head.

"What?" MaryAnn asked him.

"The truckers...think about it, Luke, Mark, and Matt? Or straighten it up, and it's Matthew, Mark, and Luke. From the East? Three of them? King Transport? Gould, Franken, and Murphy?? And they brought you gifts?"

MaryAnn just looked at Joe and didn't make any connection. Joe just shook his head and headed back to the house with the rest of the men.

*   *   *

Chapter 31

Grandma Pokes Around

The Devil is in the Details

Sarah soon brought the cradle back to MaryAnn all cleaned up and used the new blankets from the truckers to line it. She took the infant from MaryAnn's tired arms and laid the baby in the cradle. MaryAnn was exhausted, and everyone could see it. She was periodically dozing off gazing at her baby, so the women stoked the fire quietly. Grandma Agnes brought out a pot of hot tea and left it on the potbelly stovetop and left a few Christmas cookies on the nightstand. Then one by one, they all retired back to the house.

The men were already finding places to sit when the women came in. The truckers periodically looked at the big crockpot of stew that was still very full. At Farmer Harry's urging to have seconds, they dug in for another bowl and sat around talking and eating. Grandma Agnes sliced up some more bread slices, buttered one for herself, and sat back in her rocker with tea and her bread.

Joe fixed his coffee and was more than merely thankful for finding these people and this farm. He could see the soft glow of the barn lot light in the frost on the farmhouse window when "It Came Upon a Midnight Clear" began playing quietly in the background. He softly sang it to himself and was relieved that it was almost a miracle that everything worked out so well. What do I mean *like* a miracle, he wondered; it *is* a miracle! As the carol says, angels are bending to the Earth. Joe was thankful for these people and said a few prayers in his mind blessing his hosts.

Grandma Agnes had been staring at Joe for quite a while when she finally burst out loud and asked Joe if he was the father.

Shocked at Grandma Agnes' tartness, Joe fumbled his teaspoon, then regained his composure, "No, ma'am. I am the assistant to the pastor of our town church. I have been keeping an eye on MaryAnn for months now. She's had a rough life, and I help when I can. I didn't know she was with child. MaryAnn called me out of the blue and asked me to give her a ride to the store. Then she wanted me to just keep going to the city. I didn't want to drive her as I only have one headlight, but MaryAnn seemed desperate. It wasn't until we were far out of town that I figured out her problem, and it wasn't about shopping."

Joe felt foolish telling them all the details, but it was the truth as he knew it even though he was suspicious about it himself, but he didn't let on about being a bit doubtful.

"MaryAnn's mother will probably throw her out, and our church is too small to support her. Not to mention that the entire town doesn't like her, mostly because her mother's reputation is somewhat tarnished. I knew I needed to do what I could to get her some medical help. I assume she just wants to move on with her life and start over, start new. She's not eighteen yet, so I was concerned about taking her anywhere. I don't want to be arrested. But I felt it was my God-given responsibility to help her out. If she can't trust the ministers in her church, who can she trust?"

"I think you did the best with an awful situation," Jake said as he helped himself to another piece of pie.

"I'm glad I'm not in your shoes, Joe because I don't know what I'd have done," Mark said, sipping his coffee.

Harry spoke to the air with a far-away look, "You never really know when you will be called upon to do something that seems unusual. Sometimes you just have to follow the call and believe that you are doing the right thing."

*　　*　　*

Chapter 32

Grandma off Her Rocker

Rock a By the Baby

All at once, they all heard a racket coming from the kitchen. Sarah went in to see what the problem was, and the next thing they heard was Sarah shouting, "No, Grandma!" Harry and John looked at each other, then got up to go to the kitchen, where they found Grandma Agnes struggling to drag her rocking chair through the kitchen, attempting to drag it out of the kitchen door while Sarah was hanging onto the other side of the rocker trying to keep it inside.

"Ma, what on earth are you doing?" Harry asked her.

"I'm takin' my rocker out to the cottage. I have to watch over the baby while everybody is in here stuffin' their faces. If the fire goes out, the baby will freeze. I can't let that happen again."

"Let her go," Harry told Sarah. "She's got it in her mind to go babysit, so let her."

Gabe stepped up to carry the rocker out to the cottage, and Grandma Agnes shuffled quickly behind him.

Harry commented as he closed the kitchen door, "You know, I ain't seen Ma move this much in years."

As Gabe lugged the rocker to the cottage, Grandma Agnes followed behind him, "Thank you, boy. I coulda done it myself, but it's good to have some help."

"I'm glad to help, Agnes."

"I know you do," Grandma Agnes said. "I also know who you are."

"You know who I am? I'm Gabe, the farmhand," he said.

"I mean, I know who you really are," Grandma Agnes said point blank.

"Never you mind, Agnes."

"I'm not sayin' nothin'," Grandma Agnes commented.

"Okay, then maybe we can stop talking about it," Gabe said as they got to the cottage door.

Gabe placed the rocker next to the cradle, and Grandma Agnes sat with one foot on the cradle runner and one on the floor, where she could gently rock herself and the cradle.

"How is the lamb?" Grandma Agnes asked Gabe when he went over to check his charge.

"She's slow, but she's warming up. I think she'll sleep for a while."

"Good. MaryAnn, the baby, and the little lamb all need some sleep. I'm going to sit here in the rocker and keep an eye on the stove and the lamb, if that's ok."

It's okay with me," Gabe said. "Being watched over is heavenly, you know." And he went about making sure the fire was going well. Gabe saw that Grandma Agnes was already falling asleep, nearly nodding her head off. So after Gabe tucked in his little lamb, he woke Grandma Agnes and told her it was time to go to bed. He helped her get up and assisted her back to the house.

As Gabe lugged a very sleepy Grandma Agnes into the house, everyone was making arrangements for places to sleep. The truckers decided not to leave until daylight and will spend the night in their trucks. Joe will sleep on the sofa, and everyone else already had sleeping arrangements. The truckers and Joe offered to help clean up, but Sarah told them all to get some rest, and the clean-up will be taken care of.

"I'm going to check on my lamb again before I head out to the barn," Gabe said. "And I'll make sure the lantern is turned down and check the fire to make sure the cottage stays warm."

*   *   *

Chapter 33

Gabe's Reassuring Words

Fireside Chat

Gabe opened the door to the cottage quietly in an effort not to wake MaryAnn or the infant if they were sleeping. He checked on his lamb and patted her on her fuzzy head, and the little lamb looked at him through sleepy newborn eyes. He tucked her in nicely, then quietly turned down the kerosene lanterns and stoked the fire again, adding a few more small logs. As he watched the fire, he took off his hat and held it in both hands as he quietly prayed for God to protect MaryAnn, the infant, and his tiny lamb.

MaryAnn heard the prayer whispers and woke a bit. She looked over to the stove and saw Gabe from the back, and she felt sure that his hair glowed golden, but not being totally alert yet, she considered it was probably the glow from the fire.

"It's okay, MaryAnn," Gabe said quietly with his back still turned, "I'm just here to take care of the lamb and make sure the cottage is still warm."

"It is okay, Gabe," MaryAnn said, half asleep. "I have to keep waking to make sure I'm not dreaming all of this."

"Dreams can seem mighty real and make you believe they are really happening, especially in times of deep stress."

"Can you stay for a bit?" she asked. "It seems like everyone is in the house, and once again, I feel like I've been abandoned because of who I am or what I've done."

"Sure, I can sit for a bit," Gabe said as he pulled up Grandma's rocker and sat next to her. "And no, you weren't abandoned. Everyone went up to the house to eat and are now hitting the sack. You know how men are. And the women, they all think you should rest as Sarah has said you've been through a lot the past few months."

"That's true. But my life has been so lonely that it was so special for everyone here to make me feel like I'm actually human. This is like living in a dream for me. Look at you, you even care for that helpless tiny lamb. Everyone here is beyond compassionate. I love it here." Then MaryAnn asked, "So, how are you related to Sarah or Harry?"

Gabe stalled to answer that question, "I'm not related to either one, really. I came from beyond the farm. There was a time when they were in terrible emotional pain. I know they prayed so much for relief somehow. I could not help their child, but I felt I could help them get through their grief if I stayed for a while as a farmhand.

"So, how did you end up here? How could you have found this place? What do you mean beyond the farm? Are you a runaway?"

"I'm sort of a runaway." Gabe sidestepped MaryAnn's question.

"Sort of? How can you be 'sort of a runaway'?"

Gabe sighed, "Well, Harry found me in one of his wheat fields one day. He was on his knees praying for his wife and daughter. As troubled as he was with his daughter being so sick, he still took the time to take me in, feed me, clothe me, and give me a warm place to sleep. After a while, Harry understood that I have my kind of work, and he has his farm work."

"So, how long have you been here?" MaryAnn continued. "Sarah and Harry are old folks, and if they had a child die a long time ago, and you look so young, the math doesn't add up."

Gabe squirmed a bit at the line of questions from MaryAnn, but he tried to take it in stride. "Well, I guess I just have a young face," he said, then added, "I don't actually remember the dates. It seems like it's been forever ago."

"Well, I understand that. It seems like forever since the ladies at the clinic thought I might be pregnant. But you are lucky you found such wonderful people to help you out."

"Yes. Actually, I know we all helped each other. And you found these wonderful people to help you out as well," Gabe reminded her.

"You know Joe taught me that family doesn't have to be blood. It's people that love and care about each other. That's a family too."

"Joe is right," Gabe said. "You deserve a boyfriend like Joe. He appears to care a lot about your welfare, considering how he could have been liable for taking a minor away from her home."

"I don't have a boyfriend. I've never had a boyfriend. That's been the problem all along. I've never had a date, much less a boyfriend."

"I know," Gabe said, nervously twisting his hat in his hands.

MaryAnn was still talking, "I'm not pretty, and kids at

school teased me about being creepy or pushed me aside, so I kept to myself mostly. I constantly filled my aching heart with food."

"I know that too," Gabe sighed.

"You know that? How could you know that?" MaryAnn questioned.

Gabe softly spoke, "I don't think you are creepy. You have a good soul. I can see that inside. A good soul is all that matters to those who answer prayers, and a good heart makes you beautiful to those of us that can see that in people."

"Well, you could be right, or maybe what you see is from the light in the barn lot. If you saw me in daylight, you might not think the same thing. Even you, you look like you are glowing a bit too. I thought that when I first saw your hair, it is uncanny how it appears to glow."

"I am? I do? It does??" Gabe teased, combing his hair back with his fingers. "Well, you might be right about the light in the barn lot. It casts a glow on all of us. When you think about it, the light in the barn lot has brought a miracle or two here tonight."

"I hate to sound like I'm making an excuse for having this baby, but I think this whole thing is a miracle. I feel awful that I can't name a father, and truthfully I have no idea how this happened."

"It's okay, MaryAnn. Perhaps you can say the father is our heavenly father. That was good enough for one man in history."

"Oh, I don't think I'd want to lie about something like that. And I also don't think that's what happened here," MaryAnn said.

"Why not?"

"I didn't see angels or hear words in my head. In fact, I threw up when I found out."

Gabe laughed at MaryAnn's comment but spoke words of wisdom. "Giving life to a new soul is not a bad thing. Like Sarah said, it's normal, but it is also a miracle. It doesn't matter how it happened. All that matters is that you created a new life to hold a soul. That is exceptionally sacred."

MaryAnn was thinking about all Gabe had said, appreciating his kindness and wisdom. She felt like he was speaking straight to the heart of her spirit.

"Well," he finally said, "I am going back up to the house to say goodnight to everyone. It's been a long day, and I have to be up at first sun. It will be Christmas morning, you know. I'll be back to check on the lamb. She should sleep until then. Goodnight, MaryAnn." And Gabe bent over to kiss the infant, and MaryAnn saw how golden his hair was as it fell over his forehead. Again, she wondered if it was a reflection from the barn lot light shining in the window or from the glow of the potbelly stove. Gabe also bent to kiss MaryAnn lightly on the forehead. She was stunned because she could feel him from her forehead to her toes in a profoundly spiritual way. She closed her eyes to savor the feeling. When she opened them, Gabe was gone.

*   *   *

Chapter 34

Sweet Dreams

*I*t was quiet in the cottage after Gabe left except for the snapping and popping of the fire in the stove as MaryAnn wondered about what tomorrow would bring. It wasn't long before Sarah came back, wanting to check on MaryAnn and the baby before everyone went to bed. She brought a bowl of stew and was setting it on the table when MaryAnn heard her sigh heavily.

At first, MaryAnn began to feel just a sting of overstaying her welcome. "Thank you for the stew and everything," she said. "I apologize for disrupting your Christmas Eve party and being a bunch of trouble. I want you to know I'll be leaving as soon as possible."

"Oh, MaryAnn, you are not a bunch of trouble. This has been the delight of a lifetime for us. What a gift for us to have a newborn around again. You saw how touched Harry was to give the baby the cradle he worked so hard on so many years ago. Do not feel rushed to leave. Besides, it's not a good idea for you to be on the road yet. You really need a day or two to rest, or even longer. You can't be out tromping in the cold with a newborn. Trust me on that. I know what can happen to a baby in the cold. And as for you, we aren't doctors. We acted in an emergency, so we need to get the doctor out here to check that all went well. Besides, where do you think you are going to go with a new baby and your boyfriend with a pile of rust on wheels?"

"He's a friend-friend, not a boyfriend. He is the associate pastor of the town church and the only person in my town I could trust to talk to. He gave me hope when I had none left."

"Well, he seems like a good soul to us. But what matters is that you are here now and have given us all a reason to be joyous on this Christmas Eve." Sarah gazed lovingly at the little bundle in the cradle with long-ago memories of her own little bundle. "Will you be okay here tonight?" Sarah asked her. "Annie said she'd come to stay with you if you want."

"I'm sure I'll be okay. I'm tired, and the peace and quiet is nice. It reminds me of my attic room, and watching the fire makes it even better."

"Good night, MaryAnn. Sweet dreams, little mother," Sarah said before opening the door to go. MaryAnn thought she saw Sarah wipe a tear from her eye, but she wasn't sure.

*   *   *

Chapter 35

Meanwhile, Back at the House, Part Two

Something About Angels

*B*ack at the house, it is full with truckers, family, and neighbors, and Sarah felt good that she has a place for all these people on Christmas Eve. She stood there appreciating everyone and the warmth she felt from them all when Joe interrupted, "Is MaryAnn okay?"

"Yes, Joe. She'll be fine."

As talk died down, Sarah tapped her teacup with the spoon to get everyone's attention, "I wanted to tell you all that I am thrilled that you all are here tonight. Everyone found their way here because the light in the barn lot was lit. Whether you thought it was a star or a lightbulb doesn't make any difference, it was the light that was a beckoning guidepost to bring you here to celebrate this night together. When Harry and I had our child, we were so blessed, but when she died, it was a bitter, cold night like this. I never got over her death, and we never had any other children. We were so brokenhearted and lonely for so many years. So having an infant born here on this holy night that I helped bring into this world has been a true gift, the best gift. I'm glad we could be here and that our light brought all of you to us this Christmas Eve."

Sarah was done and finally, after so many years, looked at peace.

"I think it is actually Christmas morning now," Gabe said. "We're past the midnight hour."

Joe put his drink down and asked Sarah if it would be okay for him to hold a Christmas service even though he was not ordained yet.

"That would be very nice," Sarah said. "I think giving thanks for all our gifts this night would be very appropriate."

Joe got up and stood in front of the Christmas tree, looking at all the angel ornaments for a few moments before he turned to speak.

"Angels. I can't prove if there are angels as we think of them, but I believe there are angels among us. I don't think angels particularly care what faith you believe in, either. I do believe they come to watch over us or help us in a dark time. If you've been lonely and someone took time to visit with you, or you have been troubled, and someone was there that you could talk to, then I think those were momentary angels, inspired or guided by real angels. Do they take a human form to connect with us when we need to dust away gloom and fear? That I don't know. Maybe Sarah and Harry are angels for letting us in and letting us use their cottage for MaryAnn. Sarah, Harriet, and Annie are angels for helping MaryAnn bring her baby into the world, the truckers for helping MaryAnn with their gifts, Harry for giving up his child's cradle, and even Gabe for helping the lamb..."

Gabe interrupted, "Even you, Joe, driving MaryAnn to us." Sarah shushed Gabe and told Joe to continue.

"We each have gifts we don't even know we

have...listening, a hug, not judging someone, helping, understanding...all these things momentarily make us angels to another soul. So even though we may not realize it at the time, we can all be an angel for a moment. Every one of us, no matter where we came from or what our faith is, we have the ability to be an angel helper. And as we have learned on this Christmas Eve, we never know who our angels are."

A few amens were quietly spoken by the group.

Joe proceeded to tell the Christmas story of the birth of the Christ child that he knew so well.

As he unfolded the story to the group, they hung on every word as though it was the first time they heard it. He felt amazingly spiritual in this time and place. He ended with everyone reciting the Lord's Prayer. At the last Amen, he noticed Grandma Agnes with a few tears in her eyes.

"Are you okay, Grandma?" Joe asked.

"Yes, young man. I just realized this was the best Christmas service I've ever known, and I'll never have a better one." Grandma Agnes dabbed her tears with her embroidered hankie. Joe went over and gave her a hug.

As everyone began to relax, sneaking small pieces of pie or a few Christmas cookies and refilling their coffee and tea, Joe couldn't help but think about this night. He didn't dare to consider comparing the uncanny similarities with his and MaryAnn's journey of traveling to a strange place, with no room in the house, the birth of the child, three King truckers from the East Coast bearing gifts, even the tiny lamb laying down near the child. No one else appeared to have made any connection. Perhaps he was overthinking it all.

Everyone started talking about hitting the sack and how it had been an exciting yet long day. As they began to scatter, Joe told Sarah that he wanted to go out and check on MaryAnn and the baby and say goodnight.

As he quietly entered the cottage, he could see MaryAnn was well asleep, as were the baby and the lamb. Joe gave MaryAnn a quick kiss on the forehead, then kissed his fingers and pressed them lightly on the baby's forehead. "God bless you both," he whispered. "See you in the morning."

* * *

Chapter 36

The Grand Christmas Feast

The Best Gift of All

MaryAnn woke just after dawn as the women all came in bringing her breakfast and hot coffee. The three women fussed over the infant changing diapers, using fresh blankets for swaddling, and leaving clean towels for MaryAnn. MaryAnn was delighted with breakfast in bed and enjoyed seeing the three women cuddling and holding her baby. She had a brief dark thought of how her mother wanted nothing to do with babies, but she brushed it off. Not today. Her mother was not going to infect her first day, this Christmas day, with her new baby.

"It is so wonderful having a fresh new baby in the house," Sarah said while cuddling the bundle as closely as she could. "You must come up to the house and have a hot shower, then have Christmas Dinner with us, and of course, bring the little one too."

"That will be fantastic, I'd love a shower, and I'm starving even though I'm no longer eating for two!"

The ladies chuckled over MaryAnn's little joke and finished straightening up, then stoked the fire once more before they all went back to the house. MaryAnn took the time to undress her bundle of joy, re-count fingers and toes, and just gaze at the baby. She could love on this one all she wanted, and no one was going to wreck that. She knew she'd treat this little one like her grandma treated her, with love, joy, and respect, and of course, she'd sing the silly songs and lullabies her grandmother sang to her. As MaryAnn fed the baby, she quietly sang her first little song to the baby. She softly sang, "Do You Hear What I Hear? Said the night wind to the little lamb..."

Auntie Annie was elected to get MaryAnn and the baby and bring them up to the house. MaryAnn was rocking the baby when Auntie Annie entered the cottage. "Are you ready for the grand holiday meal, MaryAnn?"

"You bet!" MaryAnn couldn't get her coat on fast enough, and now that the baby belly was mostly gone, Aunt Rachel's coat almost fit. MaryAnn went ahead while Auntie Annie took her time enjoying carrying the baby. Joe saw them coming and thought that as fast as MaryAnn was shuffling over the sidewalk a couple of yards ahead of Auntie Annie, he knew MaryAnn must be starving.

As MaryAnn entered the kitchen, the smells of cooking turkey, ham, and so many side dishes were divine. She could see the dining room where the big table and side buffet were full. There were dishes piled with food all over, and wine, plates, silverware, and stemware. Everything was just brimming with goodies, like something out of a gourmet magazine. She made a passing neatness note of the kitchen being immaculate and almost nothing out of place, but with three or four women, they probably kept up with dishes.

The truckers, having spent the night in their trucks, were coming in the front door at the same time MaryAnn was coming into the kitchen. As the drivers entered, they were all talking, laughing, and joyous when Harry held his hand out to present the dining table like a casino Emcee. All they could say was, "WOW!" at the spread. Jake was there from down the road, Gabe, Auntie Annie, Harriet and her husband John, Sarah and Harry, Grandma Agnes, Joe, and of course, MaryAnn and her child. It was quite a happy holiday crowd.

Sarah led MaryAnn upstairs and gave her supplies for her shower. She said she would take her clothes and the baby's things and get them laundered. MaryAnn nearly melted at the supreme sensation of the hot water washing her icky past life down the drain. Whatever was in the shower water on this farm, MaryAnn felt like it magically soothed her. She wanted to stay in the shower until all the hot water was used up, but she also wanted to get down to dinner. MaryAnn was drying her hair when Sarah returned with her laundered clothes.

"Thank you, Sarah, this is really a welcome treat. The shower was triple awesome, and thank you for laundering my things." MaryAnn wondered how on earth her clothes were laundered so quickly, but she was too excited about dinner to worry about the details. She dressed and hustled downstairs.

When MaryAnn entered the room, everyone stopped, and one by one, they congratulated her with handshakes and joyful hugs. MaryAnn could feel the acceptance and joy from everyone. With an especially warm, tight hug from Gabe, he whispered, "Merry Christmas to you both, and may God bless you and keep you." He then kissed her cheek. MaryAnn felt momentarily overcome by his touch and looked at him as he went to the dining table to find his place. He glanced back at her and simply smiled. His hair seemed especially golden, but right now, food was ready, and everyone was busy choosing their roosting places around the table to be seated. For so many, there were just enough seats, and everyone fit perfectly. Harry spoke as things quieted down, "As head of the house, I usually say Grace, but I'd like to confer that honor to Joe today, as he was the one that really brought us all together in a way."

As a light applause broke out from everyone, Joe nodded his acceptance. He actually wore his clerical collar for the holiday under his MIT sweatshirt, even though he never went there.

"Nice sweatshirt, Joe!" Mark playfully said when Joe stood. "MIT is impressive!"

"Oh, well, it's not the college," Joe said as he looked down at the letters for a second, then he looked up and said, "It stands for Minister-In-Training!" Laughter erupted from everyone.

Joe bowed his head and began by thanking the hosts for opening their home to MaryAnn and himself and also for hosting the truckers. He explained that nearly everyone sharing what they had was one of the greatest blessings anyone could receive. He thanked God for these fine people and their kindness, then gave thanks for everything on the table and asked for blessings for everyone. And lastly, he thanked the light in the barn lot that brought them all together. Joe finished with a heavy sigh and "Amen." It was followed by everyone agreeing. Amen.

"Dig in, everyone, before it gets cold," Sarah instructed, "We don't have a microwave to reheat!"

Suddenly it seemed everyone was starving with all the reaching for platters and bowls of food and passing everything every which way. There was lots of laughter, silverware clinking on plates, sharing of food, and plenty of wine with toasts all around. Sarah and Harriet made MaryAnn drink milk, but they poured it into wine stemware. MaryAnn looked around at the happy people. Just hours ago, they were all strangers, and she was miserable, but here she was at their table, adoring them all and feeling exquisite joy. She'd never had a holiday dinner where no negative words were spoken. Her eyes welled up with some momentary emotional tears when she realized she didn't need packages to open or gifts to make Christmas special, just this gathering of good people was enough. Christmas couldn't possibly be any better.

Out of the blue, Grandma Agnes' voice was heard shouting her crotchety voice over the dinner sounds, "What are you going to name the baby?"

A polite quiet fell over the dinner as all eyes looked to MaryAnn. MaryAnn looked at each person and knew how much she loved them all right now, knowing everything they did to help her and her baby, but she didn't want to commit to tagging a name just yet. "Well, it's all been so exciting and new that I haven't decided yet. I'll have to give it some good thought."

Mark responded, "Here! Here! A toast to MaryAnn, and whatever name she chooses will be perfect!" Everyone held their glasses up and toasted MaryAnn while MaryAnn held up her glass of milk. MaryAnn felt overwhelmed. She'd never known the feeling of being adored by so many and strangers yet...and no one commented about her looks at all. For once, MaryAnn considered that perhaps her looks really didn't matter to good-hearted people. She filled her plate with all kinds of fabulous food, and nobody looked or made an unkind remark. It was so pleasant to eat without criticism, and the food was delicious.

*   *   *

Chapter 37

$\mathcal{M}$ysterious $\mathcal{G}$abe

Who is He?

$\mathcal{M}$ost of the afternoon was spent with everyone around the table having second helpings, then pie and coffee, and lots of conversation. Everyone brought different stories and experiences to the table and there was plenty of laughter.

Toward sunset, MaryAnn was growing tired and needed to feed the baby. She hated leaving such a wonderful day, the best day of her life, but she wanted to excuse herself to go back to the cottage. Gabe volunteered to go along to check on the lamb and make sure the stove was stoked well for the evening.

As they walked back to the cottage, MaryAnn asked Gabe, "What happened to the lamb's mother?"

"Nothing. She's fine. But the barn gets too cold for the weaker newborns, so we keep them inside overnight. If the sun comes out tomorrow, she'll go back to her mother."

"I'm glad. I know babies love to be with their mothers."

"Yes, they sure do."

As soon as they got to the cottage, Gabe began

warming a bottle for the lamb. She let out a few bleats waiting for her bottle. MaryAnn watched the young man tenderly care for the lamb and carefully stoke the stove again. She remembered that he said he'd been working at the farm for a long time, and he seemed to act older, but his face was so young looking and pale. She thought a farmhand would have a more rugged look and tan. But being winter, maybe he lost it. And now, in the late afternoon light, she still couldn't get over his golden hair.

Gabe sat in the rocker with the bundle of lamb and fed her the bottle while MaryAnn was nursing her baby. "This is so odd, us feeding the little ones," MaryAnn said.

Then out of the blue, Gabe spoke, "I'm older than you think, a lot older."

"Did I ask that?" MaryAnn asked.

"You didn't have to. I knew you were thinking about it. There is no explanation that you could understand of my existence."

"But you work on this farm, don't you? Where did you live before here?"

"I've been where I've been called to work."

MaryAnn was becoming aware that Gabe was either crazy or had too much time alone in the barn with critters. So whether he was fourteen or forty, it didn't really matter to her, as he was warm and wise, and it just felt good having him in the same room. MaryAnn was becoming aware that she was feeling a little smitten with the guy, or maybe it was something else. She wasn't sure. He always looked at her like she was special, but he looked at everyone that way.

Gabe interrupted her thoughts again. "You know I can't leave here. I'd love to go with you and be a fill-in father to your little one, but it can never be. I have a different path

I'm bound to follow."

MaryAnn was shocked at his comment. She'd only had a single passing thought about maybe she could eventually hook up with Gabe but blew it off, knowing that wasn't reality. After everything she'd been through with her mother, she was well aware that we live in the real world, not the dreams in our heads.

Gabe finished feeding the lamb, and she had fallen asleep in his arms, so Gabe laid her in her corner on the blankets. Then he sat on the edge of MaryAnn's bed and lovingly pushed her hair from her face. "You have a beautiful heart and soul. Love the child above all else. Grace and beauty will find you. I will always be watching over you both." And he leaned over and kissed her on the forehead. "I gotta get back to the barn and check on the others. I hope to see you before you go. I know you are going tomorrow morning. You need to make a call; someone is worried." And Gabe left the cottage, his golden hair reflecting the setting sun.

MaryAnn could feel his kiss for some minutes, like warm electric tingles, and how did he know she was leaving tomorrow morning? She never mentioned wanting to go. But she did want to go. She wanted to get a cell phone connection so she could call Aunt Rachel and tell her the good news. She knew Aunt Rachel would be very worried by now. Then it dawned on her that Gabe mentioned she should make a call and that someone was worried. He must be psychic, she thought. It was then that MaryAnn became excited about showing her baby to Aunt Rachel.

MaryAnn was exhausted from the anxieties and stress of everything from the past few months, plus a huge dinner. MaryAnn couldn't help nodding off. She had sweet dreams of living with Sarah and Harry, raising the baby on the farm in the clean air, with good food, and getting to know Gabe better until a knock on the cottage door aroused her. Joe stuck his head in, "They are getting sandwiches out for a night snack. Are you interested, or do you want me to bring you something?"

"Thanks, Joe, but no, I'm stuffed still from eating all day."

"It was good, wasn't it?"

"I'll say. I'd like to move in with these folks if dinner is always that spectacular."

"I know. You could probably stay here, but I need to get back to the church. I left a note on my desk that I had to run an emergency errand, but I sure thought I'd be back for the Sunrise Christmas service. I don't know if Pastor Bob will send the bloodhounds looking for me or not. Maybe Sarah and Harry will let you stay for a while; if you want."

"I don't want to stay, Joe. I want to call Aunt Rachel so she's not worried. I also want to take the baby to show Aunt Rachel. I looked around when I was up at the farmhouse, and they don't seem to have a landline phone. I don't think there is cell reception here anywhere, either. Do any of them have cell phones? I think we'll have to drive up on a hill someplace to make a call."

"Well, we'd better plan on getting out of here early tomorrow. My cell phone battery is just about shot. I asked around, but nobody seemed to have a charging cord. And Sarah and Harriet were talking like you should go to the doctor to make sure everything is okay with you and the baby. They said medical folks will check you and the baby for the important stuff; besides, you need to fill out the information for the birth certificate. The baby will need that. You know how important the paperwork and filing are." Joe winked at her with his little joke.

"I suppose they are right, Joe. I guess it'd be best to get directions to the city. If we can find a clinic or an ER, I'm sure they can do the necessary stuff. Lots of babies are born, so I'd think everyone would have the stuff to make sure I'm okay."

"Then it's settled. We'll get directions and head out of here tomorrow right after breakfast. I'll go talk to Harry and let them know our plans."

MaryAnn gave the baby a tight hug, "Oh, you little sweet pea, I can't wait to show you to Aunt Rachel!

*   *   *

Chapter 38

Saying Goodbye is Hard

Grab Your Coat and Get Your Knitted Cap

*M*aryAnn woke with a start just before dawn, hearing the loud racket of engines starting up and the ground rumbling. She jumped out of bed, washed up, and got dressed to go see what was happening just as Gabe came in.

"You are up early," she said to Gabe.

"It's going to be a sunny day, MaryAnn, so the lamb gets to be with her mother today. I heard you are heading out too. The truckers are checking their loads and warming up their engines now. They'll be leaving in a few minutes too. It's going to get quiet around here real fast."

"I'm sorry, Gabe. Sarah thinks I need to be checked out by a doctor, and I want to call my aunt, so she stops worrying."

"Yes, you need to call her. She is worried." Gabe gently picked up the infant from the cradle and used his finger to trace a cross on the baby's forehead. "May the Lord bless you and keep you, and lift his countenance upon you and give you peace."

"That was very sweet, Gabe. I'll miss you, you know."

"I know," Gabe said, then opened his arms wide, "Come here."

MaryAnn stepped into Gabe's open arms and received the gentlest warm hug she'd ever known. "The Lord bless you and keep you as well," he said, then kissed MaryAnn on the forehead. MaryAnn felt dizzy and faint momentarily from the emotional stirring from Gabe's brief touch. It wasn't passion; it was more of a beloved feeling, so different and fulfilling. She was sad it was time to say goodbye, but somehow she knew deep down that it had to be this way.

They said their goodbyes as Gabe picked up his bundle of burlap and lamb and left the cottage. MaryAnn watched him as he walked nearly all the way to the barn, watching his glowing blond hair ruffle in the breeze. She tried hard not to cry. Then Sarah came in with breakfast.

"Ahhh, good timing Sarah. I'm so hungry."

"Joe told me you are leaving today. Harry wrote down directions to the city and the hospital there. They are nice folks and will help you. Harry also wrote down where he'd be able to pick up a cell signal so you can make your calls. I'll be sad to see you go. It's been so eternally long since we've had a baby around. I've thoroughly enjoyed you being here and wish you'd stay. We'd have plenty of babysitters for you."

MaryAnn thanked Sarah for everything, but she wanted to get back to her Aunt. Sarah understood and was just glad she could help where she was needed. "It was amazing as I had some kind of premonition that something wonderful was coming. When Joe knocked on the door, I was almost waiting."

Sarah and MaryAnn gave each other big hugs, then Sarah picked up the baby and sat in the rocker humming a lullaby while MaryAnn finished packing. They heard the truck engines all fired up and start to move out. "I should have gotten addresses for them so I could send them thank-you notes," MaryAnn said.

"Oh, I should have told you; they gave me their names and addresses. I wrote them down, and I'll get the note for you when you leave. I'm sure they know how much you appreciated the gifts they brought," Sarah said while cooing and babbling to the baby.

MaryAnn finished her breakfast and was finished packing her things to go. She was teary-eyed about leaving her new family but knew she had to make things right with Aunt Rachel and make sure she got the medical all-clear. She had to admit that the stomach nausea was totally gone. So maybe this was all a good sign.

Joe came out to the cottage to get MaryAnn's things. "Are you ready?" he asked. "I'm sure when we get back to town, I'm going to have some explaining to do. Sarah and Harriet wrote a letter to Pastor Bob explaining why I was missing. Maybe it'll help keep me from being fired."

"Omigosh! Can they fire an assistant pastor?"

"I think so. But I think the gist of the whole letter was not to implicate me as a kidnapper and that I was just assisting you in getting medical help.

"Sheesh. Yes, getting back to town is going to be interesting. I sure hope I don't get you fired."

MaryAnn followed Joe back up to the house, but Sarah was slow coming with the baby. It was time to say goodbye. The goodbyes were laden with plenty of tears but also plenty of smiles. So many thank-yous, so many hugs. Sarah cried more than all of them, and MaryAnn seemed to know Sarah was missing her child all over again. I now understand the pain of losing a child, MaryAnn thought.

Grandma Agnes stood looking at MaryAnn for a few moments until MaryAnn gave her a loose hug goodbye. Grandma Agnes didn't hug MaryAnn. She kept her hands behind her back. As MaryAnn stepped back, wondering if she did something to upset her, Grandma Agnes sheepishly brought her arm around, holding a white hand-knit stocking cap for the baby. "I can still knit. It's been eons since I've knitted anything, but I wanted the baby to have something. I started that cap back when...." Grandma Agnes stopped and looked at Harry and Sarah before she finished the sentence. Sarah nodded okay, and Grandma Agnes finished, "...when Sarah was pregnant. I'm glad I could remember how to knit so I could finish it today. And I'm glad that someone can wear it now."

"Awwww, Grandma Agnes, this is so sweet of you. Thank you so much," MaryAnn gushed. The cap was charming, and MaryAnn put it on the baby's head while Sarah held the bundle of infant. Sarah broke down and cried.

"I'm so sorry, Sarah," MaryAnn said.

"No, it is fine. It is the way it is supposed to be," Sarah said, wiping tears away. "This is a happy moment. I can one last time remember what it was like when our daughter was born. It's a gift."

There were more hugs and tears than you'd see at the end of a family reunion, but it was now time for Joe and MaryAnn to go.

As they got in Joe's car, leaving was bittersweet for both of them. They all waved at each other as they drove back down the gravel driveway and kept tossing waves until the farm and its family were finally out of sight.

MaryAnn sighed, and Joe checked the directions on the note he got from Harry about how to get back on the highway. "Looks like we will be in the city in about forty-five minutes. I sure hope they can see you at the medical center right away. On one hand, I'm itching to get back to the chapel, on the other hand, I think I could just keep driving and forget about going back to face the music. I see trouble ahead at the hospital about the paperwork and more when we get back to town."

*   *   *

Chapter 39

The Road Back to Reality

Strange Coincidences

*A*s they drove, MaryAnn cuddled her baby as a new adventure was in the works.

When they got to the little hill that Farmer Harry indicated they'd get cell reception, Joe got a decent signal. Joe called Pastor Bob, but he wasn't in his office, so Joe was glad to leave a message that he was okay, tending to a patron, and would be back tomorrow. MaryAnn quickly called Aunt Rachel. Aunt Rachel was relieved that MaryAnn was okay and irritated that MaryAnn didn't tell her that she was leaving. Knowing the cell battery was dying, MaryAnn only had a moment to quickly explain having Joe take her to the city, but they got lost and ended up at a farm of very nice welcoming folks where she had the baby. MaryAnn and Aunt Rachel had a short discussion about MaryAnn coming home with an infant and Aunt Rachel said she'd be thrilled if they'd come to stay with her, at least for now, until they could try to explain it to MaryAnn's mother. MaryAnn, happy to be asked to stay with Aunt Rachel, thanked her and explained that she was on her way to the city hospital to be checked out. The call ended just before the battery gave up.

"Well, that's a load off both of us," MaryAnn told Joe.

"Yes, for now, anyway. When everyone gets the details, they will certainly assume I'm the father," Joe said.

"I suppose we can do a DNA test that will prove you are not," MaryAnn suggested.

Joe brightened up. "Good idea! I believe that is right. We might have to do it a couple of times for the townspeople who love to gossip, though. They'll think we fixed the results."

"I know. I wish I didn't have to go back there. I now realize how beautiful life can be when you are around gracious people. Gabe was so wonderful. It felt so good to talk to him and just be near him."

"I know. He was up at the house a few times, and I could tell he was a good soul," Joe said.

"Did you ever notice how pale he was, and his hair was so blonde it nearly glowed?"

"Yes, I noticed it too but didn't want to make a deal out of it. It'd sound odd coming from another guy."

"I suppose you are right," MaryAnn said, cracking a bit of a smile

As the car approached a small intersection, Joe slowed, "Ahhh, this is the road to turn on. We went the wrong way here. This will put us back on the highway, and we should be only about a half hour away from the city and the hospital. I hope they can see you quickly so we can get back home before they send out search parties."

As they rode, MaryAnn couldn't take her eyes off her baby. Joe kept glancing at her. He could see how in love she was with the little one. On one hand, he was happy for her to have found some love in her life. However, on the other hand, he was still slightly troubled about who the father was. On the third hand, he didn't know if he should bring it up that the medical facility will ask her that exact question. He shivered when he momentarily thought that she might pin him with being the father. Who would believe him? But again, MaryAnn was right; DNA would absolve him from any fatherhood.

Joe kept thinking back on all the coincidences of this birth as he drove. First and foremost MaryAnn swore there was no hanky-panky before she found out she was pregnant. She was ostracized by everyone. She had no money. There was no room at the farmhouse, so she was ushered to a cottage out back. Then, holy cow, the three King truckers from the east, even if it was New Jersey. Who is to say where in the east kings were to come from? Their names, can that be a total coincidence? Gould, Franken, and Murphy? Even their first names; Matthew, Mark, and Luke! The lamb lying down with them. Even the fact that her name was MARYAnn. He yelped a bit out loud when he also realized his name was Joe. They were ridiculously similar to Mary and Joseph.

"Jeeeeeeez!" Joe exhaled out loud.

"What's that about?" MaryAnn asked. "Are you fed up with me by now?"

"No, just think, have you considered all the coincidences we have encountered since the day you came into the church?"

"Coincidences, what coincidences??"

"Everything!" Joe said, then he went on to explain all his thoughts about how close all the events mirrored a certain popular holy night."

MaryAnn stared out the front window. "No way. It can't be. It's just coincidence."

They both rode in silence for some minutes before Joe spoke. "I can't believe it! Who would believe it? I was there, and I scarcely believe it."

"This is my baby, and I don't feel anything unusual. I feel love, but I don't think this was any special birth or special child."

"How would we know if it was?"

MaryAnn's face clouded over as she thought about that.

Joe went on, "You know they will ask you who the father is. And if you are truthful that you don't know, they might say you were raped or drugged or lying. You are going to have to endure some pretty rude comments from people in town when they find out. In an out-of-wedlock birth everyone wants to know who the father is. You've seen the birth information at the church; there's always a father mentioned, married or not."

"Well, I've already endured plenty of rude comments from kids and some of their parents in my life. How much worse can it get?" MaryAnn snuggled her baby closer. "Would the town be willing to gather DNA to prove paternity? Something must have happened. This cannot be a fatherless birth. It's scientifically impossible."

Joe thought about that. "I'm not so sure everything has to be explained in science. As a man of faith, I have to say that sometimes we must take things on faith. Just because you can't see the wind, doesn't mean it doesn't exist, it leaves its effect that you can feel. Besides, I don't see the people in town interested in sticking their necks out for a DNA test to be ruled in or out. And if it were to come back as no one local is the father, they'll just say it was someone passing through the area or when you stayed with your Aunt Rachel."

MaryAnn knew he was right and thought for a moment, then quietly and calmly commented to Joe, "So, do you believe a virgin birth would be possible? They say it happened once. There has always been hope in the world for another one, right?"

Joe's arms went numb at the thought. "Oh God, MaryAnn, I can't even wrap my head around that. It would be impossible to explain it to anyone these days. Talk about ridicule! You'd get and screams of fake news! Not to mention it would be considered sacrilegious by most people.

"Well, isn't that what happened to Mary's mother or something? Didn't they throw rocks at her?"

"That was Mary Magdalene. I think. I'm so confused by all of this that I can't even think straight!"

MaryAnn sat looking at the passing landscape, then sighed, "It is just too ridiculous. It has to be something else, plain and simple."

Joe agreed. "Let's just say, for now, that you don't know the father, which is the truth, but I suspect they'll press for more details."

"Gabe mentioned something kind of out there about wanting to step up to act as the father, but he said he couldn't leave the farm for some reason. I should have asked him if I could name him as the father, at least for now. He was such a sweet person that seemed to have a real interest and concern about the baby."

"Well, you need some kind of plan for what you are going to say when they ask you about the father. Systems are digital now. They'll need answers."

As they turned onto the interstate, the signs indicated the city was eighteen more miles.

*   *   *

Chapter 40

Behind the Double-Door

A Future from the Past?

*J*oe drove in through the ER entry drive and dropped MaryAnn off so he could park. By the time he got back to the building, MaryAnn had already been swept into the inner sanctum of the ER department. When he asked about her, they refused to tell him anything as he was not related. He kicked himself for not lying to them and telling them he was her uncle or brother or something. He wouldn't dare say he was the father. He knew that would end up in the paperwork somewhere. He also hated lying about anything. So he sat in the waiting room worrying about MaryAnn being underage by a day or two and worrying that they'd have the cops come after him for kidnapping a child. He sat and worried for nine eternities from hell. He was going to get coffee from the machine but knew the caffeine would just jumpstart more anxiety, so he sat with his leg jittering non-stop, holding his head in his hands. He had a passing thought that the waiting room should be called the worry room.

Eventually, just before lunch, MaryAnn appeared through the double doors in a wheelchair with a cheerful volunteer shoving her along with her bundle of infant clutched to her chest.

"Wow, that took forever," Joe said.

"I'm sorry, they wanted me to fill out papers for insurance and other stuff, and I don't have insurance. They wanted my next of kin and I don't want my parents contacted. They kept asking me who the father was and didn't want to release me until I gave them the father's information and the baby's chosen name. I told them the circumstances of having the baby at a farm. They asked for that address, but I really don't know. I said, you might know, so they let me out to talk to you for a minute. I lied and told them I was eighteen. They made me swear it, as I don't have any photo IDs to prove it. So I'll have to ask you for confession later. I still have to go back to finish filling out the papers and the state department of statistics before I am released. Other than that, we both checked out just fine. The baby is healthy, and I'm good too."

"Wow. Well, if they won't let you out of here without a father, just give them my name. We can clear it up later. We'll say you were under duress at the situation with your mother being so hateful and the weather and all. They might buy that since most of it is true."

"I don't think that's a good idea. Once the town finds out about the baby, they'll be digging for evidence against you, and it'll be on the record. I'll see if they'll let me put "unknown" down. Maybe I'll tell them I'm afraid to name the father."

"I mentioned it casually before, but maybe you could tell them it was our Heavenly Father. He's the creator of us all. They probably won't want to get in a squabble with you over that."

"I don't want to even think about lying about God." MaryAnn hesitated a moment and felt a warm, calm envelope her, then said, "I have a strange feeling I should give them Gabe's name for some reason. Gabe said he can't leave the farm, so maybe they'd never be able to follow up. He did briefly comment about considering himself for the job."

"Maybe he wouldn't mind. But I'm not so sure. If something happens to you, they'll hunt him down as the baby's next of kin or maybe try to get child support from him."

"I doubt anything is going to happen to me for a while. But come to think of it, I didn't get a last name of any of the people on the farm, so how could I use his name as the father?"

"Well, maybe just tell the truth. He was a farmhand to that farm, so what about Gabe Farmer?"

"Hmmm... that might work. I suppose if they want to track him down, I could give directions to the farm. I just don't recall an address."

"Well, that long driveway was off East-West Post Road. Just write that it's rural. Like Rural Route 1, East-West Post Road, that should work. I doubt they are going to mail him anything anyway."

The volunteer pushed MaryAnn back through the double doors to the lady with the paperwork. After some paper shuffling, they finally released MaryAnn. Joe and MaryAnn nearly ran out of the hospital before anyone had any more questions. They were both glad to be on their way home.

Both were quiet for a long time on the drive as they both reviewed the memories of the past two days.

At the place where the turn-off was to Harry and Sarah's farm, MaryAnn told Joe that she'd like to go back to the farm and thank them for everything. And she felt it was her duty to tell Gabe what she did on the paperwork.

"Yes, Gabe should know. Until that's posted in the department of vital statistics, you can still change it if he doesn't want his name there. We can't stay long. I have to get back to the church."

"I know. And Aunt Rachel is expecting us for supper. By the way, she mentioned bringing you too."

"Oh, I don't know about staying for supper, MaryAnn. I'm sure Pastor Bob will be looking for me and want to question me about my whereabouts on Christmas day."

"I think he can wait a little longer. I know I can get Aunt Rachel to call Pastor Bob and explain that she wanted us both to come for supper. You can explain the details to him after you get back to the church and give him the letter from Harry and Sarah."

"Under the crazy circumstances, I hope he will understand. I think he will, as he is aware of your situation with your mother."

They got to the road that led to the long gravel driveway that led around the corner to the farm. MaryAnn was excited to see everyone again as they continued up the driveway crunching over the gravel. As they drove around the last turn in the driveway, MaryAnn shrieked almost loud enough to wake the baby.

"Oh, my living God!" Joe said as he stopped the car, folded his arms over the top of the steering wheel, and stared at the sight ahead.

*   *   *

Chapter 41

Ashes to Ashes, Dust to Dust

All that is left

*A*s they came upon the farm, all they could see that was left was a pile of age-old ruins and an overgrowth of weeds and small scrub trees. There was hardly anything left that hadn't rotted to the ground. Even the rock structures had fallen into disrepair and crumbled. MaryAnn was stunned at the sight.

As Joe looked at the ruins, he was nearly in shock. "This has to be the place. It must be."

"It can't be," MaryAnn said through tears. "This makes no sense. All of this has rotted to the ground into heaps of broken-down rubble. It looks like it was never a farm. I am so confused."

They drove into the barn lot that was lightly dusted by snow that covered the piles of dead weeds and the smattering of long weathered ruins. There was a rotted wooden stump where they thought the barn lot light was. A few rocks were still piled up from the foundations, and a small portion of one of the enormous barns remained, but the other buildings were time-worn piles of deteriorated wood and rusted tin roofing that had collapsed in. The once white fences were tumbled down peeled paint, weather beaten, and fragmented.

"What on earth happened here?" Joe said. "It looks like it was bombed. This is the farm we were at hours ago? There's only one dilapidated silo still standing and a part of the barn Gabe lived in. The rest has crumbled to the ground. And look, there is just a bit of a foundation spot where the cottage was!"

MaryAnn and Joe looked at the ruins and were bewildered. They both got out of the car to see if this might be the wrong place. They were hoping it was. How could this have become such a pile of run-down debris in the few hours they were gone? And where did the people go?

"Where are Sarah and Harry? And Grandma Agnes?" MaryAnn said as she picked her way through the long-decayed rubble and debris. "This can't be right."

They looked at each other, and both said at the same time, "And where is Gabe?"

MaryAnn poked through the remnants, some of which were frozen to the ground. Then she saw something. "Wait!" MaryAnn shouted to Joe, "Look, here's a piece of a plate." She dug it out of the frozen ground and rubbed some clay and dirt off with her thumb. "This is the same pattern that was on Sarah's dining table just yesterday." MaryAnn held it, then began to cry again. "What is happening, Joe?"

"I don't know. I'm going to try to figure it out," Joe said as he picked up a stick and began to poke around the rotted boards and rocks from the crumbled farmhouse. It was barely a few minutes when Joe shouted, "Oh my God, MaryAnn, check this out." Joe dug a little something from the shallow dirt. "This sure looks like Harry's pipe. It makes sense, he kept it on the mantle, and this is the foundation for a fireplace."

MaryAnn was dumbfounded. "What could have

happened here?" MaryAnn said, sniffling from tears as she picked through the remains. "This was all so beautiful just a few hours ago. What does it mean? Where are Sarah and Harry?"

As they rummaged through the wreckage, they saw an old woman nearly limping up the road. She was bundled up and clumping over the gravel wearing men's galoshes with the buckles loose and clinking. Joe fixed his clerical collar so he wouldn't frighten the old lady, and he waited for her to slowly shuffle up the drive to the barn lot.

"Good day," Joe said.

The old lady looked at Joe and over at MaryAnn that was wandering in the rubble, picking up bits and pieces and looking at them. "I saw that car yonder headed up the drive. I wanted to check and see who was up here messin' around the old foundations." The old lady looked at Joe, saw his collar, and felt comfortable talking to the stranger.

"It's okay, ma'am," Joe said. "We thought we were here just yesterday, but it doesn't look like the right place."

"No, I didn't see nobody here."

"Do you know what happened to the big farm that was here?" Joe asked as he looked over the land.

"Farm? Oh, that hasn't been a farm for over a century. Nobody seems to know who owns it. A few people have wanted to buy the land over the years, but it never seems to sell."

"We were here just yesterday," MaryAnn said as she walked up to the two. "We had a huge Christmas dinner with the farmer and his wife, his family, and some other people. It was a wonderful day."

The old lady looked at MaryAnn like she'd lost a marble or two. "You sure this is the place? There's been nothing here but the ruins for many years, decades. The story was that more years ago than anyone can remember, it was a beautiful storybook farm for a farmer and his wife. They were young and worked their farm, and were very faithful. They finally had a child, but the child sickened from the flu. They prayed hard for days on end, but the child went to be with the Lord." The old lady bowed her head.

MaryAnn repeated, "But we were just here yesterday! We saw the light in the barn lot from out on East-West Post Road, and we came here. I stayed in the cottage, we had a big dinner, lots of food, people, the farm hand, the little lamb at the cottage, even three big trucks rolled up into the barn lot....." MaryAnn trailed off.

"I'm sorry young lady, it can't be. There's no barn lot light here. Heck, there ain't even any electric. There's been no light here for over a hundred years. You can see how it is, and it's been this way all my life. I've lived down the road for over 80 years, and my parents before that. My grandfather Jacob bought the land in the 1800s. He lost his wife pretty young, but he stayed on to raise his three boys. One of them was my father, who told me he used to get in trouble with his father for playing up here in the rubble. His father thought this land was sacred or something. As far as we know, it has always been abandoned. I never saw any of these buildings before they collapsed in."

MaryAnn appeared to be in shock. Joe was just endlessly scratching his head and running his hands through his hair. Then he asked the old woman, "Did you hear three tractor-trailers rumbling up here Christmas Eve?"

"I think you might be just yankin' my chain. No, there's been no trucks or any other kind of traffic. I don't sleep much and can hear really well, so I don't even miss a coyote howl off in the distance. I'd have heard a four-wheeler on the gravel, not to mention a semi."

Joe stood there looking at the old lady. She sure looked like she was being right with him. MaryAnn was still staring mindlessly at the wreckage. They both couldn't possibly have imagined everything that happened here.

Joe thanked the old lady and sent her his blessings. "Well, thank you, ma'am. We won't keep you from your walk."

"That's all right young man. Enjoy being a father, Father."

Joe cringed at her comment, but as he watched the old lady shuffle back to the road, he told MaryAnn, "This is weird. I can see from the placement of the house foundation and some of the other buildings that this is laid out exactly like when we left this morning. Even the barn lot light pole stump is there. I was not dreaming all this."

"I know," MaryAnn agreed. "Wait..." MaryAnn said and rushed back to the car and grabbed something. She returned in a few seconds waving a white knitted cap, the note from Harry, the letter to Pastor Bob from Sarah and Harriet, and Sarah's list of addresses from the truckers. "Look, this is the cap Grandma Agnes knitted and gave me just a few hours ago. I'm not imagining this, nor imagining the things we dressed the baby in that the truckers brought. Or the ton of food we ate. Or even the directions Harry gave you."

Joe glanced at the note MaryAnn was waving at him. "Wait, let me see that note," he said. He took the note and flipped it over, looking at both sides. The paper was fine, but the directions Harry wrote were not there. All Joe had was a plain piece of blank paper. Joe kept checking the paper on both sides while MaryAnn opened the envelope to Pastor Bob. Just like the note, it was just paper, no writing. Same blank paper from Sarah's addresses. MaryAnn and Joe looked at each other stunned.

"How can we have the paper but not the writing on it?" MaryAnn asked.

"How would I know? I don't know what to say, MaryAnn," Joe said. "This is like some kind of weird backward miracle dream. Maybe we were hypnotized. The story the old lady just told us matched what Sarah and Harry told us. It was obvious that they were devastated by the death of their child. And the old lady said her grandfather was Jacob, that lost his young wife, so maybe that was like Jake, the widower guy. Did those events lead to some kind of emotional residual impression on the farm? Something like haunted, but in a heavenly way? Then again, we saw it. The farm was here when we drove up. It doesn't make any sense."

Joe walked to the stump of the light pole and looked for remains of the light, but none was there. He did notice some tire tracks in the snow. "Check this, MaryAnn, look, big tire tracks, like from a huge truck. There's another over there too. It looks like a couple of big trucks were here recently. If these belong to the truckers, were they in on the dream too? And how could that old lady miss the racket those trucks made coming and going? They rumbled in so loud that the coffee in my cup had waves in it."

"I don't know. I heard one of the truckers say they'd never gotten lost in all their years of driving. So why now?"

They both continued to walk through the rubble, trying to understand what happened, but nothing was adding up.

Joe finally gave up. "None of this makes sense. We both believe we were here with these people for two nights, Christmas Eve and Christmas Day. We had great company and wonderful food, and it has suddenly vanished?

"Now that you mention it," MaryAnn added, "it was strange with all the food on the table. Nothing appeared to be cooked in the kitchen. Who cleaned up while I was out in the cottage?"

"I don't know. I never saw anyone cleaning up. I don't even remember anyone cooking. I was busy talking and eating stuff. I asked if anyone had a phone I could use or a charging cord, and I never saw one. Come to think of it. I never saw much of anything working. For a farm, I didn't see any machinery like tractors, mowers, plows, balers….and other than the lamb, no animals."

"Me neither. When I walked through the kitchen, I didn't see food out, nor containers or pots and pans."

Joe added, "You are right. I don't recall appliances or a refrigerator or anything. I hate to keep saying it, but it doesn't make sense. They must have had electricity. There were lights on, the Christmas tree was lit, and there was an extension cord going out the door of the cottage that lit up the little tree." Joe thought for a minute. "You know what? Something else was strange, now that I think about it. Even though the place was lit, I didn't notice lamps or anything other than the strings of Christmas lights on the front porch and the Christmas tree. It seemed like everything was lit from within somehow."

"Oh, come on," MaryAnn said, "I saw at least one big crock pot on the buffet in the dining room."

"Yes, but did you see it plugged in? And that crockpot never seemed to empty for as many bowls that were dished out. Did you even see if there were plugs and light switches?"

"Well, no," MaryAnn said. "I was in the cottage most of the time, and I only had two kerosene lanterns and the potbellied stove. It was a nice light, though."

"Okay, well then, how did we see that light in the barn lot if there was no power? How was that lit?" Joe was quiet for a minute, then spoke softly, "I'm starting to wonder if it was some kind of mystical lure to get us here."

MaryAnn picked up a piece of broken tile, "This is the tile that was in the shower, same unusual pattern. I stood in that shower for the longest time. I couldn't mistake this tile. Sarah took my clothes....." MaryAnn stopped, collecting her thoughts.

"What?" Joe asked.

"Sarah brought my clothes and the baby's things back laundered, dried, and clean. How did she do that in the short time I was in the shower?" Joe just kept shaking his head in wonder.

Suddenly MaryAnn noticed something moving out in the field of winter wheat, a faint flash of light from the sky to the field that produced a slim length of pale prism light, like a piece of a rainbow from a summer storm and a wave of the golden wheat. She shielded her eyes from the sun to get a better look. As the image began to form, the prism faded, and she could see what looked like a person.

*   *   *

Chapter 42

Gabe

Transcendent Inspiration

$\mathcal{M}$aryAnn squinted hard in the daylight, and as the person came closer, she could see golden hair reflecting in the early afternoon light. It was Gabe.

MaryAnn ran into the farm ruins, followed by Joe as Gabe held his arms open to receive his friends. "Gabe! What is happening here??" MaryAnn said as she hugged Gabe.

Gabe hugged them both for a few minutes, then looked at MaryAnn. "We didn't expect you to come back."

"What? But I wanted to come back and thank everyone for their time, their gifts, their help, their love...." MaryAnn trailed off and considered what she would say next about putting Gabe's name on the birth certificate.

Gabe spoke before MaryAnn even started her sentence. "It is okay, MaryAnn. I know you put my name on the baby's register. I think you may know why now."

"No, I don't think I do. And how could you have destroyed all that was here?" MaryAnn asked. "Why was it all demolished?"

"We didn't do anything to it, time did," Gabe explained. "This was a beautiful farm long ago. The way the farmer lived his life, caring for the farm, his family, the land, the crops, and the animals, was benevolent and faithful. Because he glorified all things as sacred, his land became hallowed and graced with a heavenly radiance that shimmered over the farm, and the land became sanctified. It still is. It's kind of like walking on holy ground."

MaryAnn looked at her shoes and stepped back a few steps, "Holy ground?"

"Well, not exactly, but you should know this blessed place called to you so we could give the gifts of so many that were prayed for. That the Farmer and his wife lost their beautiful little girl after praying so hard for her. They wanted another child so badly, but it never happened until you came along. Their souls got to relive that joy. There were truckers that wanted to celebrate Christmas traditionally but couldn't when they were on the road every year until you came along. There was a grandma whose heart was broken when her little granddaughter sickened and died, she started to lose her faith, but she could see that child smile in her dreams and finish the cap when you came along. A man from down the road was miserable during Christmas after his wife died from cancer, but he was able to enjoy Christmas once again. An assistant reverend wanted to help people, and he did when you came along. A lonely girl prayed for someone to love and someone to love her in return, and she wanted true faith to believe in, so we answered the prayers, and the petitions were granted...."

Gabe held out his palm toward the infant bundle on the seat of the car. "We answered. We answered the prayers. We answered your prayers. We put a gift of light out for you to see and to follow after we got you to get off the highway. You should know that prayers are not always answered as direct as the prayees would like. Sometimes they are answered in spiritual ways that you cannot always understand how or why when it is happening."

MaryAnn looked at Joe in disbelief. Joe was already in his world of stunned awe.

Gabe continued, his soft melodious voice soothing both MaryAnn and Joe's sense of shock. "I know this pattern of events may seem familiar, but it is what we know. It has passed the test of time for so many eons and across distant horizons, and this is how it is done. You were becoming unhopeful in so many ways. We heard your prayers and helped you find the light in your life and uncover your faith in yourself. Faith must start within you. We saw you losing your faith in yourself, so we brought a rare and transcendent star down from beyond the everlasting to guide you to us so we could bestow the gifts of faith and love through hope, belief, and miracles. It all comes to those who Believe."

MaryAnn was still in shock, her head buzzing with conflicting information.

Gabe could see MaryAnn's hypnotic trance and wanted to soothe her distress. "I kept something for you," he said, hoping to spark MaryAnn's attention back from wherever it was stuck. He fished something out of his coat pocket and carefully put it MaryAnn's hand and folded her fingers lightly over it. It was only a few seconds when MaryAnn's eyes opened wide, and she looked down into her hand. There she saw an angel cookie cutter. She stared at it in total incredulity while Gabe said, "You never know how your prayers will be answered."

MaryAnn whispered, "This was the one on my tree? In the cottage?"

Gabe nodded.

"Then all this really did happen? The people were here? There was a beautiful farm and cottage?"

Gabe nodded.

MaryAnn thought for a minute, then spoke, "Who are you?"

Gabe began, "I would have never told you, and we thought once you left the farm that you wouldn't look back and you'd be living your real life. But perhaps we should break a small rule. You call me Gabe, but most faithful and spiritual souls know of me as Gabriel, one of the divine messengers. If you look me up, you will see that I am one of the guardian angels permitted to walk the physical world to guide, protect, and inspire. I am the celestial attendant designed to help you on your destined path." Gabe stopped suddenly and looked back at the wheat and the sky, "I cannot stay. I have to go now. There are many others waiting for their time."

Joe's jaw was hanging open like he was waiting for an airplane to land on his tongue, still not really grasping what was happening. MaryAnn could only thank Gabriel and held his hands in hers, then kissed him on his cheek. "I think now I understand why you said you go where you are needed. Thank you for being here with me. Thank you for helping us. Thank you for hearing my prayers and giving me such a wonderful gift. If there are others, thank them too. Thank you for your grace, guidance, and inspiration as well. I will always remember you."

Gabriel took MaryAnn's face in his two hands, and she could deeply feel his benevolent spirit working into her soul as though they were both momentarily one. "You are beautiful," he whispered to her, then lightly kissed her on the lips before saying, "And thank you." He looked so deep into her eyes that he could see into the recesses of her heart and saw it was joyful.

Joe was beyond speechless at what he was witnessing and blankly shook hands with Gabriel. Gabriel said, "What the heck, Joe," and Gabriel pulled him in for a big man-hug patting him loudly on his back. Joe had big tears rolling down his cheeks. "Remember what I told you at the farmhouse the night the child was born, Father Joe,"

Joe nodded, his emotions somewhat shook-up.

Gabriel began to walk back to the fields but stopped and turned to Joe, "Preach what you have learned and what is now in your heart, and know that to believe is to be blessed."

Joe nodded again and wiped away a few tears with his coat sleeve. Gabriel then spoke to MaryAnn, "Take good care of the little one." He kept walking a few steps, then stopped again, turned to them both and said, "See that piece of tin roofing over there? Look under it. Please take it with you. They want you to have it. Goodbye, MaryAnn. You'll see me again one day and in your dreams."

"With that, Gabriel kept walking until he entered the golden field where his golden hair blended with the winter wheat, and in a pale flash of prism light, he was gone. MaryAnn sniffled a bit, knowing deep down that she would not see him again for a long time.

"Did we just talk to an angel?" MaryAnn asked Joe through her dewy eyes. Joe was still staring. "Joe? Joe??"

Joe finally gathered himself together, "What?"

"I asked if you think we just talked to an angel."

"I don't really know. I sure thought we had Christmas at a farmhouse with regular folks, but now I don't know where the heck we were. Here? Heaven? Some other dimension? I don't even know if we went back in time or something. Who were those people? Ghosts? Memory energy? Angels? Even in my position, I never once considered what seemed like a regular guy could be an angel. I guess we don't know who or what our angels look like that cross our paths in life. And apparently, if we let them, they can lead us to places that answer our prayers. What a lesson. When I become an ordained minister, I will preach what Gabriel has taught me."

"Gabriel said there was something under that big piece of tin. Let's go see if we can dig under it."

Joe climbed over the clutter until he got to the piece of roofing and pushed the big piece of tin up with his stick." Oh, MaryAnn, I cannot believe this. Look!"

MaryAnn picked her way through the debris to peer under the tin. There they both saw the rusted, collapsed remains of what was once a pot belly stove, and next to it was the nearly perfectly preserved gift of love and dreams.

The hand-carved cradle.

"Oh, Joe, they saved the cradle that Harry made." MaryAnn fell to her knees and broke down in tears.

Joe knelt with her and supported her in his arms. He now understood how he was needed so much more than just as a ride to the city.

After wiping some tears out of both their eyes, the two were able to dig the cradle out from under the section of rusty roof and other debris that had covered it. The cradle was half filled with dirt, leaves, and rubble as though it had been sitting for a hundred years, yet MaryAnn thought she had just taken the baby out of it earlier that morning.

After they wrangled it out of the ruins and knocked off most of the dirt, Joe put it in the trunk of his car while MaryAnn scoured the landscape to see if she could see Gabriel somewhere in the fields.

"It's in the trunk, MaryAnn. Are you ready to go?"

"I don't know, Joe. I feel like I belong here, with those people."

"I don't think they were people, MaryAnn."

"Oh, come on, they weren't goats or sheep. They were people. I hugged them, they fed us, we talked, and they birthed my baby, for crying out loud."

"I think they were spirits of those that lived here many years ago. Their spirits were so strong, and their memories so vivid that they could create that dreamlike place. This was the place they knew where their worst memory seemed to stop them in their lives. Their hearts stopped...not the beating, but they stopped because they were so broken. And according to Gabe, or Gabriel, they had a sense that you were coming; and bringing the little one. They were going to be able to relive a joyous time in their lives and, perhaps once and for all, put the painful past behind them. So they lit the light in the barn lot. I was right the first time we saw it, and it looked like a star. It was a star. They brought it down from the heavens for us to follow.

Joe pulled MaryAnn in for a hug. He looked up to the heavens and said, "Perhaps, if we look up in the night sky tonight, we can see the star. Gabriel will point it out for us somehow. You must teach your child to look for that star and tell the story of the light in the barn lot."

*   *   *

Epilog

Keep the Faith

So now, dear reader, you've read the story. True? Believing is up to you. We all have to ask ourselves if there is something more in the divine realm than we can understand, something that calls to those in desperation, something that may light a mystical celestial passageway along a guided path for the faithful to follow. Do we have to be willing to let go of our preconceived notions to surrender to those dreams? Is it all a coincidence, or is it a miracle of belief? Do we blindly go forth with trust in our hearts or ignore the call? Choices are made every day. And you know MaryAnn and Joe made theirs.

Upon returning to Aunt Rachel's farm with the baby, Aunt Rachel was over the moon with the newborn bundle of joy. MaryAnn stayed with Aunt Rachel and helped with the vineyard, and Aunt Rachel helped with the baby. The baby grew in the fresh air and loving hearts of MaryAnn and Aunt Rachel. Eventually, MaryAnn told Aunt Rachel the story of what happened that Christmas Eve and about Gabriel. She went on to explain that she wasn't sure who the father was but said she wasn't interested in uncovering something that no one would understand, so she declined DNA testing.

Rita, MaryAnn's mother, did not want to participate in the baby's life. Rita kept her distance and spent more and more time at Jerry's Gin Joint and at the Brown Lobster and kept drinking. She eventually died in her sleep from over-intoxication.

After her mother's death, MaryAnn inherited her mother's house, but she sold it and most everything in it. Too many unpleasant memories, MaryAnn said. She boxed up her collection carefully and put it in storage, not feeling like she needed plastics and ceramics to help her believe in herself anymore. Her mother had eaten up much of the equity getting loans against the property to support her party life and her perpetual quest for youth. Still, enough was left to help MaryAnn get settled. Aunt Rachel gave her a plot of land on her farm so that MaryAnn could build a small house of her own.

MaryAnn's father had remarried in the city and made rare visits to see MaryAnn and the child.

Pastor Bob went easy on Joe under the circumstances. Joe never told him any details about going back to the farmstead after the hospital visit, or about Gabriel, or what he and MaryAnn witnessed. He could barely believe it himself.

MaryAnn and Joe kept in touch for a couple of years and visited often. Joe enjoyed watching the baby grow, and the child loved Joe's attention. MaryAnn regularly had Joe over for dinner, usually beef stew in the crockpot and homemade bread. They always seemed to end up talking for hours about their shared mystical experience.

It was a few years later that Joe and MaryAnn married, and Joe became the Reverend at a community church across the county line. They remained a happy family of three in the little house on Aunt Rachel's farm. Many evenings they walked together on the farm, often hoping to see Gabriel appear in a field, but they knew he was working to help others find their own Peace on Earth.

On any given December night near Christmas, MaryAnn and Joe would sit out under the twinkling night sky bundled in blankets looking up for their guiding star with joyful hearts remembering Gabriel and the people they met from the other side. And snuggled tightly between them, their child with the unusually golden hair would say, "Mommy, Daddy, tell me the story again about the star in the barn lot and the night I was born."

Merry Christmas.

Thank you for reading my book.

www.ingramcontent.com/pod-product-compliance
Lightning Source LLC
Chambersburg PA
CBHW030225180626
46810CB00008B/2976